Robin Hood

A Play

by Don Nigro

A SAMUEL FRENCH ACTING EDITION

SAMUEL FRENCH

FOUNDED 1830

New York Hollywood London Toronto

SAMUELFRENCH.COM

ISBN 978-0-573-69051-8   Printed in U.S.A.   #20075

CHARACTERS

Alan a'Dale
Sheriff of Nottingham/Sam the Rag
Constable Watt/Eadom o'the Blue Boar
Gill Redcap/Mitch the Miller
Diccon Cruikshank/Cootie the Drunk
Robin Hood/Blind Benny
Little John/Dumb Duggan
Davey o'Doncaster/Arthur o'Bland
Will Stutely/Sir Stephen
Will Scarlet/Deaf Danny
Friar Tuck
Prince John/Bell the Tinker
Yorick/Grok/Flint the Beggar
Dark Monk/Purvis the Peddler/Richard/Ghost

Maid Marian
Lady Quigley/Old Maid of Tuxford
Bronwen/Maid of Tuxford/Sister Felicity
Queen Eleanor/Old Maid of Tuxford/Prioress
Sally Serving Wench/Gwenny
Ellen Dear/Maid of Tuxford/Brekka
Jenny Brown/Maid of Tuxford
Crazy Betty/Old Gummy Granny/Old Maid of Tuxford

SETTING

Mythological Medieval England. All locations present at once — the players may bring on and carry off tables, rocks, etcetera from scene to scene if necessary. The songs are meant to cover transitions — see the music at the end of the script.

"Then arose the famous murderer, Robert Hood, as well as Little John, together with their accomplices, from among the disposed, whom the foolish populace are so inordinately fond of, celebrating in tragedy and comedy."

—Johannis de Fordun, *Scotichronicon,* 15th century

Robin Hood was originally commissioned by Mark Cuddy, Artistic Director of the Idaho Shakespeare Festival in Boise, Idaho, where it was first produced in the summer of 1984 with the following cast:

Alan a'Dale	Dan Green
Grindl the Idiot Girl	Erin Corday
Sheriff of Nottingham/Sam the Rag	Tony Carreiro
Constable Watt/Eadom o'the Blue Boar	Dan Peterson
Gill Redcap/Mitch the Miller	Tedd McClellan
Diccon Cruikshank/Cootie the Drunk	Clay Wilcox
Robin Hood	Douglas Copsey
Maid Marian	Laura Jones
Blind Benny	James Henderson
Little John	Tim McDonough
Dumb Duggan/Will Stutely	Don Schlossman
Davey o'Doncaster/Arthur o'Bland	Jonathan Chaus
Sir Stephan	Ralph Lucas
Sally Serving Wench/Gwenny	Kirsten Giroux
Deaf Danny	Gavin Kirkpatrick
Will Scarlet/Lame Louie	Thom Allen
Friar Tuck	W. Allan Batchelder
Prince John	Wayne Cote'
Queen Eleanor	Pam Abas
Lady Quigley/	
Old Maid of Tuxford	Carole Whiteleather
Bell the Tinker	Brian Powell
Yorick	David Lee-Painter
Jenny Brown/Maid of Tuxford	Kim Gillingham
Brekka/Crazy Betty/	
Old Gummy Granny	Lisa Raquel Klein
Prioress/Old Maid of Tuxford	Terri Morgan

(continued on following page)

(continued)

Grok/Flint the Beggar . . . . Tom Willmorth
Ellen/Old Maid of Tuxford . . . . Gina Scorsone
Dark Monk/Richard/Ghost/Purvis . . . . Peter Griffin
Bronwen/Maid of Tuxford . . . . Carissa Channing
Sister Felicity/Maid of Tuxford . . . . Toni Redman

Directed by Mark Cuddy. Scenic Design by Jeffrey Hunt. Costume Design by Bitsy Bidwell. Lighting Design by Jonathan Langrell. Fight Choreography by David Boushey. Makeup and Hair Design by Nancy Harms. Additional musical arrangements by David Miller. Assistant Director, Paul Frellick. Stage Manager, Laurie Baker. Assistant Stage Manager, Patricia Knowlton. Fight Captain, Tony Carreiro.

ROBIN HOOD

ACT ONE
Scene 1

Sherwood Forest. Bird sounds. ALAN sings, to one side, with lute:

ALAN.
HOW MANY MONTHS IN A YEAR MY LOVE?
THERE ARE THIRTEEN, I WOULD NOT LIE—
BUT THE SWEETEST MONTH IN ALL THE YEAR
IS THE MONTH ONE DOES NOT DIE.

(As he sings, MARIAN appears, followed by QUIGLEY, THE SHERIFF, CONSTABLE WATT, and the soldiers, GILL RED-CAP and DICCON CRUIKSHANK. GILL labors carrying an enormously heavy picnic basket for MARIAN, who is determined to be cheerful. Everybody else is nervous.)

ALAN.
TWAS ONE FINE DAY IN A TIME LONG PAST
WHEN THE SHERIFF AND HIS MEN
IN THE FOREST DARK HAD LOST THEIR WAY
WITH THE FAIR MAID MARIAN,
WITH THE FAIR MAID MARIAN.

7

MARIAN. Oh, isn't this charming? So primeval. I do adore the forest so — grove and copse, thicket and coppice, furze and gorse, scrubwort and bulrush — isn't it beautiful?

QUIGLEY. It makes me itch.

MARIAN. Let's have our lunch right here. *(GILL in some relief puts the basket down.)*

SHERIFF. It's much too late for lunch, milady, and we shouldn't stray so distant from the horses and the baggage. *(GILL dutifully picks up the basket again.)*

MARIAN. Sheriff, I will not consume lunch while horses perform body functions in close proximity to my potato salad. *(GILL puts the basket down.)*

SHERIFF. But we mustn't stop, milady, seeing as how we may not exactly know for certain that where we think we are is not in fact the place we ought to be. *(GILL picks up the basket.)*

MARIAN. Does that mean we're lost?

SHERIFF. Lost? Oh, no, milady, we're not lost, lost are we not, oh, ho ho, no, lost? Us lost? We? Lost?

MARIAN. I take it that means yes. *(GILL sits down, basket in his lap.)*

CONSTABLE. Do not fear, milady, for I never in my life was lost, even the time I run into a tree on a night as black as me first wife's rump-hair, and didst stagger headsfirstwise WUNK into a bog-hole, smellt like the place cheese goes to die, but I wasn't lost, for they did nose me out from a mile or three distant, on account of the sumphole stench was all about my person, so I was found comparatively quick, though I was not too popular for a fortnight after, except with me brother's pig which fell enamoured of me and had to be sold.

SHERIFF. Then where exactly are we?

CONSTABLE. Same place we was half an hour ago. In fact, we been here several times today.

SHERIFF. You mean we've been going round in circles?

CONSTABLE. No, sir, we've just been coming back to the same location.

SHERIFF. I think you're right. I recognize this place.

CONSTABLE. Then you're not lost, are you?

SHERIFF. But where exactly are we on the map?

CONSTABLE. Oh, we ain't on the map, we're in the forest, you can tell by all the trees.

MARIAN. Wherever we are, I like it. Look at all the May apples.

SHERIFF. They're poison, milady.

MARIAN. Not to look at, I hope.

SHERIFF. I tell you, this be not a safe place to stop in.

MARIAN. If you don't know where we are, how do you know if it's safe or not?

QUIGLEY. Are there bears? I'm deathly fraid of bears.

REDCAP. Bears?

CRUIKSHANK. Easy, Gilly.

CONSTABLE. Me uncle Dob was et by a bear in the wood, twas a tragical thing, let me tell you. He'd gone off to do what no man could do for him, and the bear smelt him out. It was sad.

SHERIFF. There are no bears in these parts. Wolves, maybe.

REDCAP. Wolves?

CRUIKSHANK. Steady, Gill. There ain't no wolves. Though I did hear once that a Dark Monk creeps through the forest here, with a death's head for a face, drags you off when it's time to die.

SHERIFF. It isn't spooks or wolves that we need fret about — it's outlaws.

REDCAP. *(holding his head and mouthing in terror)* Outlaws?

CONSTABLE. We found parts of me uncle scattered through the woods — the bears dropped bits of him along the way like a trail of breadcrumbs. That's how I got me lucky finger, I keeps it in me pocket always, except when bathing. See? *(He shows an embalmed finger to QUIGLEY.)*

QUIGLEY. That's a nice one.

MARIAN. Surely no outlaws in the world would be foolish enough to attack the Sheriff of Nottingham, and Constable Watt, and Prince John's finest soldiery.

REDCAP. Where?

CRUIKSHANK. I think she means us, Gill.

CONSTABLE. Oh, it's true, milady, we doesn't want to be hangin about here too long, or we may be hangin about indefinitely, like hams from the trees, for the robbers may jump out of the bushes at any time and slash yer throat from one ear to tuther straight across like a sack of wheat, and for the first thirty seconds you was dead, you'd never know it, they does it so neatly.

SHERIFF. Watt, be still, you're alarming the ladies.

MARIAN. I'm not a bit alarmed. I'm supremely confident that you and your men can protect us from outlaws, bears, panthers, crocodiles, or anything secreted in the wildwood. Now, who would like a ladyfinger?

QUIGLEY. Perhaps if there are crocodiles and bears we should go on.

SHERIFF. There are no bears.

QUIGLEY. There might be bears.

SHERIFF. Milady, I swore to Prince John I'd get you safe to Nottingham by sunset. It's lunacy to stay in these woods after dark, for here the outlaw Robin Hood does lurk, a bloody murderer with many desperate men.

MARIAN. My Papa says, if you're lost in the woods, just stay put, and somebody will come along and find you. Hug a tree.

CONSTABLE. Your father hugs the trees? That's awfully strange.

OLD LADY. (Bursting upon them from the woods with a blood-curdling cry.) AAAAAAAAAAAHHHHHHHHHHHH-HHHHHHHHH. (REDCAP and CRUIKSHANK jump and scatter. QUIGLEY tries to hide in the picnic basket. The CONSTABLE runs into a tree. The SHERIFF draws his dirk. MARIAN is slightly ruffled but recovers quickly.) OH, LORDY, IT BE PEOPLE, IT BE UDDER HUMID BEANS, OH, THANKEE LORDY, I BE SAVED. (She is stooped and covered with a hood and a long dress, and she runs about hanging onto them one by one.)

SHERIFF. Pull yourself together, woman.

MARIAN. Don't be cross with her, she's upset.

QUIGLEY. She's a dirty peasant woman, milady, you don't want to be touching her, the hoof and mouth is going round again.

MARIAN. Oh, rot. What's the matter, dear? Have you

had a fright? Have you fallen on bad times?

OLD LADY. And on me arse. Oh, missy, I been so frighted.

QUIGLEY. Is it bears?

OLD LADY. It's outlaws, missy. I been ravished, and ravished again, and ravished once again, I been ravished so many time I've lost the count.

CRUIKSHANK. *(aside, dry)* These be desperate outlaws indeed.

QUIGLEY. Just whereabouts ARE these outlaws?

OLD LADY. Oh, they ravished me upside the one side o the glen and downside the the other side o the gilly, and up and down the dingle they did it, it was terrible to see, it was that awful Robin Hood.

REDCAP. I knowed this was goin to be a poor day when I stepped out of me trundle bed directly into me thundermug.

SHERIFF. Are you certain it was Robin Hood?

OLD LADY. Carved his initials on me backside, do you want to see?

SHERIFF. He's still close by then?

OLD LADY. Oh, sir, he's nearer than you thinks, I knows it, and I'm so frighted I can barely hold me water, oh, don't let them at me, sir. *(She has clutched onto the the SHERIFF and is hopping about in circles with him.)*

SHERIFF. Here. Madam. Control yourself. GET THIS FILTHY WOMAN OFF ME. DOWN, WANTON.

CONSTABLE. Here, missus, let the Sheriff go, now, we'll protect you from them outlaws. Come on, fellers, help me here—

(While they are occupied with this, they are being quietly surrounded by Merry Men who appear one by one from behind trees and such: DAVEY, LITTLE JOHN, WILL SCARLET, WILL STUTELY, ALAN, and FRIAR TUCK last, with a hiccup.)

CONSTABLE. Here now, listen, madam—

WILL SCARLET. Take your hands off that woman, Sheriff, she's too good for you.

CRUIKSHANK. *(looking around)* Oh, begob, we're in for it now.

REDCAP. OUTLAWS! HELP!

SHERIFF. Silence, you ninny. I see Will Scarlet, and Little John, and all the rest of you, but where is that coward Robin Hood? Does he dare not show his face near the Sheriff of Nottingham?

OLD LADY. Near you? Sweetie, I've near been ravished by you.

(She whips off hood and wig to reveal ROBIN HOOD. In his own voice:)

ROBIN. You really ought to bathe more often, Sheriff, you'd meet a better class of people if you did.

REDCAP. *(Pulling his hat down over his head, hysterical:)* ROBIN HOOD! IT'S ROBIN HOOD' *(Much screaming and confusion as the outlaws descend upon them. A loud, mad battle. QUIGLEY screams and runs back and forth. MARIAN tries bravely to help. The picnic basket ends up over the CONSTABLE'S head. The SHERIFF'S party is routed, leaving MARIAN and QUIGLEY surrounded by the outlaws.)*

LITTLE JOHN. What a fearsome group. Lookit 'em go.

Looks like a marathon race.

ROBIN. Ladies, your escort seems to have left without you.

QUIGLEY. *(Pleading on her knees to LITTLE JOHN.)* Oh, don't hurt her, sir, she's a poor virgin, at least that's what she says, and I for one believe her. If you must ravish somebody, ravish me.

LITTLE JOHN. *(not too thrilled at this prospect)* Do I have to, Robin?

MARIAN. If you mean to do us harm, I warn you, my father is a rich and powerful noble.

ROBIN. Is he? And just how much money has your noble father got?

MARIAN. I can't discuss my father's finances with a murderer in the forest.

ROBIN. Then don't bring it up in the first place. What are you doing out here, anyway?

MARIAN. I'm on my way to Nottingham to marry Prince John. *(The outlaws burst into laughter. She is indignant.)*

ROBIN. Is that what he told you?

MARIAN. What do you mean, is that what he told me? Why are they laughing?

ROBIN. I don't want to disillusion you, but Prince John is not the most trustworthy fellow in the world at this— *(He takes a casual step towards her and she jumps back.)*

MARIAN. Don't come near me or I'll kill myself.

ROBIN. And how will you do that?

MARIAN. I'll stab myself with my brooch.

DAVEY. No, I got your brooch, miss. *(He holds it up.)*

MARIAN. Give me that back, you savage.

ROBIN. Now you behave yourself. I can't very well let you have sharp objects if you're going to impale yourself with them, now, can I? This savage with your brooch is Davey O'Doncaster—

DAVEY. Yo.

ROBIN. And this bluff fellow here is Will Stutely—

WILL STUTELY. At yer service, miss.

ROBIN. And this handsome devil's Will Scarlet—watch out for him—

WILL SCARLET. I am charmed beyond reason.

ROBIN. And this dainty thing is Little John—

LITTLE JOHN. *(shy and mountainous)* Please to know you.

ROBIN. And that's Alan a'Dale, our minstrel—

ALAN. I'll make a song for you, miss, if you like.

ROBIN. And that distinguished-looking gentleman grazing on the remains of your picnic is Friar Tuck.

FRIAR TUCK. *(Waving a roast chicken at her.)* God bless you, my child. *(He belches.)*

ROBIN. And I am Robin Hood, the bloodthirsty savage, and you are Maid Marian Rose, daughter to Sir Stephen of Trent, and her companion Quigley—you see, even out here in the forest we know one or two things. Now, what we've got to ponder is just what we savages are going to do with you. What do you think, men? Shall we disembowel them?

WILL SCARLET. I'd like to kiss her first.

ROBIN. I don't think she wants to be kissed. At least not yet.

MARIAN. I demand that you release us immediately.

ROBIN. I can't very well set you loose here in the middle of Sherwood Forest. The Sheriff himself was lost, and he spends a good deal of time lurking about in these parts. How do you expect to find your way home?

MARIAN. We'll risk it.

ROBIN. Yes, but I won't. They'll say I've murdered you, and I prefer being guilty of what I'm accused of. Let's see—we could sell you to the Welsh—no, I like the Welsh. We could feed you to Frair Tuck.

FRIAR TUCK. Sorry. Gave up cannibalism for Lent.

ROBIN. Well, that's out then. I suppose you'll just have to come back to camp with us until we can puzzle out some convenient way of disposing of you.

MARIAN. I refuse categorically to move from this spot.

ROBIN. That spot right there?

MARIAN. Absolutely.

ROBIN. All right then. Little John, you get the old one and I'll take this one myself.

LITTLE JOHN. Lord, I do hate this. *(He slings QUIGLEY over his shoulder like a potato sack.)*

QUIGLEY. AAAAAAAAHHHHHHHHHHHHHHHH.

LITTLE JOHN. Gor, Robin, it's like carryin' a horse to church.

ROBIN. So, who's next? *(He moves toward MARIAN.)*

MARIAN. I'LL GO. I'LL GO. Just keep your hands off me. Lady Quigley, are you all right?

QUIGLEY. I'm attempting to faint, milady, but it's difficult with all the excitement.

ROBIN. Get the rest of this baggage, lads, and bring along the horses. Come on. Hup, hup. *(LITTLE JOHN staggers off with QUIGLEY. Others scatter to get the baggage. To*

MARIAN:) Go on, SCOOT. SHOOOOO. *(MARIAN scuttles off after LITTLE JOHN with as much dignity as she can muster.)*

WILL SCARLET. She's a comely one, ain't she, Robin? I like 'em spirited like that, don't you?

FRIAR TUCK. A fair maid is the devil's playground, boys, you keep that in mind.

WILL SCARLET. I'll try. But I'll fail.

ROBIN. Did you hear that? Listen. A kind of odd piping sound?

WILL SCARLET. I hear nothing. See, already the woman's got you going daft. Come on Friar, don't eat the basket. *(TUCK and SCARLET go off. ROBIN lingers a moment listening, then follows.)*

ALAN. *(Singing, to one side.)*
WHAT DO YOU HEAR IN THE WOOD MY LOVE?
WHAT MAKES YOUR FACE SO WORN WITH
  CARE?
I SAW MY LOVE ALL DRESSED IN WHITE.
I HEARD THE LEAVES A WHISPERIN THERE
THAT DEATH IS A SONG SO SWEET MY LOVE,
THAT DEATH IS A SONG SO SWEET.

Scene 2

Nottingham castle. PRINCE JOHN brooding, depressed and surly, watching an extremely elderly and enfeebled jester, YORICK, try to stand on his head. By his side sits his ancient mother, Queen Eleanor, formidable and perhaps asleep. His mistress BRONWEN is having her toenails painted by SALLY SERVING WENCH, a very nervous little creature.

BRONWEN. *(observing YORICK)* He's going to hurt himself, you know.

PRINCE JOHN. I know, but it amuses Mother to watch him fail.

BRONWEN. I don't think she's amused, I think she's dead, she hasn't moved since Thursday.

QUEEN ELEANOR. *(measured and chilling)* I shall frolic upon your grave, you disease-ridden cow.

PRINCE JOHN. Be nice, Mother.

QUEEN ELEANOR. The day grows more lugubrious by the hour. Tell him to astonish me.

PRINCE JOHN. Come on, Yorick, mother's getting bored, the new wench is late—do something funny. Yorick? Yorick? *(YORICK has his head on the floor and his legs partially bent in an aborted headstand, and is presently not moving.)*

YORICK. *(snoring)* ZZZZZZZZZZZZZZZZZZZZZZZZZ.

BRONWEN. He's fell asleep again. How does he do that, right in the middle of it?

PRINCE JOHN. You fall asleep during intercourse.

BRONWEN. Not standing on my head I don't.

PRINCE JOHN. WAKE UP, YOU IDIOT. *(He boots YORICK on the backside, and the jester falls over, flop.)*

YORICK. *(Screaming pathetically as he falls.)* AAAAA-AAAAAAAAAAHHHHHHHHHHHHHH. *(SALLY jumps at the sound.)*

BRONWEN. Hey. You've painted my foot.

SALLY. *(trying to wipe it off)* Sorry, mum.

PRINCE JOHN. Come on, Yorick, do something funny, right now, or Mother shall be very cross with you, won't you, Mother?

QUEEN ELEANOR. You have intercourse standing on your head?

BRONWEN. Yer makin' it worse, me foot's all purply. *(SALLY rubs harder.)* OWWWW. I'll do it, I'll do it. *(SALLY starts to cry.)*

YORICK. *(on the floor)* Funny?

QUEEN ELEANOR. I don't think I ever tried it on my head.

PRINCE JOHN. Funny. You know. Jokes. You remember jokes.

QUEEN ELEANOR. I thought I'd tried everything.

BRONWEN. Don't cry. Go make the Queen some hot toddy. Go on.

SALLY. Yes mum. Thankee mum. *(She scurries out, nearly running into the door on her way.)*

YORICK. Jokes?

PRINCE JOHN. *(Dragging him up with some trouble.)* Get up, or we'll ship you back to Denmark.

YORICK. Oh, yes, what? Oh, I have a jest. Oh, yes. This one be a genuine loin-slapper. You see, a certain fellow doth think to peruse an afternoon in a tavern, whence he cometh to quaff sack, and, in a mood to have much merry jest, doth leap manfully upon a table— *(He tries to illustrate with a manful leap upon a table, falls on his face, then rolls over, table and all, upon the floor.)*

BRONWEN. He never could do that

YORICK. *(trying to get up and continue)* —it's quite all right, fear not. And this same fellow didst proceed to open up his codpiece, and lo, and behold, he hadst secreted into this codpiece a bird of the duck variety, which protrudest its head from said codpiece in the midst of said jesting fellow's pantaloonst— *(Trying to brace himself with the table and right it at the same time he overbalances and flops over it onto the floor, the table now on top of him.)*

QUEEN ELEANOR. We should have this man put to sleep.

(The SHERIFF enters, somewhat uncomfortable.)

SHERIFF. Um, your majesty, sir—

PRINCE JOHN. Don't bother me, I'm attempting to amuse myself.

SHERIFF. Sir, I think you may want to know this—

PRINCE JOHN. Come on, Yorick, come on, boy, you can do it, get up, upsy daisy, attaboy, good dog.

YORICK. *(struggling up to his knees)* So this merry fellow hast the head of yon duck protruding from the codpiece of his pantaloonst, and cometh bounding towards the serving wench and ordereth hearty usquebaugh, and a plate for the birdie. And as the merry fellow quathed the usquebaugh, he did put—um—he did put—

QUEEN ELEANOR. Corn.

YORICK. Eh?

QUEEN ELEANOR. Corn. He put corn in the dish.

YORICK. What dish?

QUEEN ELEANOR. For the duck, you imbecile.

YORICK. Duck?

SHERIFF. Sire, please—

PRINCE JOHN. All right, all right, but I'm warning you, this had better be good news.

SHERIFF. Well, sire, it's actually, uh, RATHER good news, partly. That is, the escort for Maid Marian has got safely through the forest and is arrived at the castle. I led it personally.

PRINCE JOHN. That IS good news. Excellent, Sheriff. Where's the wench? When can I see her?

SHERIFF. That, sire, is a small part of the news which is perhaps not quite so good.

PRINCE JOHN. What? Is this bad news? Have you brought me bad news?

SHERIFF. Not really BAD news, sire, exactly—

PRINCE JOHN. Doesn't she want to see me?

SHERIFF. Oh, no, sire, I'm certain she'd love to see you, it's just that you can't see her quite yet.

PRINCE JOHN. Yes I can. I'm the Prince. I run the realm, I rule the roost, I am the chief goose of the gaggle, the Queen's representative on earth, I can see her any time I want to.

SHERIFF. Except when she isn't here.

PRINCE JOHN. Well, of course I can't see her when she isn't here, I'm not the Holy Ghost, that's why I want you to bring her in here, so I can see her.

SHERIFF. But that's why you can't see her, sire.

PRINCE JOHN. What have you brought me? An invisible woman?

SHERIFF. No, sire—

PRINCE JOHN. THEN WHY CAN'T I SEE HER?

SHERIFF. Because she isn't here.

PRINCE JOHN. I KNOW SHE ISN'T HERE, THAT'S WHY I CAN'T SEE HER.

SHERIFF. Exactly.

YORICK. What duck?

PRINCE JOHN. The duck in the fellow's codpiece, that was eating the corn, in the dish, in the alehouse. For God's sake, you've been telling this joke since William the Conquerer played patty-cake, can't you get the damn thing right for once?

YORICK. Oh, yes sire, I remember it, hee hee hee, it's a good one, yes, hee hee, the old washwoman is watching from the corner, see, and she spieth the duck's head protrude from the said fellow's codpiece, and nibble thusly at the corn in the dish, and the woman saith—hee hee—hee hee hee—HIC—he heee—HIC—

BRONWEN. Got the hiccups again. I knew that was comin.

YORICK. HIC. HICCCCCC.

PRINCE JOHN. Listen to me, Sheriff, did the escort reach the castle safely or didn't it?

SHERIFF. Yes sir, it did.

YORICK. HIC.

PRINCE JOHN. Then why can't I see Maid Marian?

YORICK. HIC.

SHERIFF. Because while the escort did in fact reach the castle safely, Maid Marian did not.

YORICK. HIC. HIC.

PRINCE JOHN. WHAT DID YOU DO, FORGET HER?

YORICK. HICCC.

SHERIFF. She was captured, sire, by Robin Hood and his men.

YORICK. HIC.

PRINCE JOHN. ROBIN HOOD? CAPTURED BY ROBIN HOOD?

BRONWEN. Good for him.

YORICK. *(Trying to cure his hiccups by putting a bag over his head, but now choking and gagging in the bag.)* HIC. HIC. HIC. GGGGGLLLLLLGLGLGLGLGLGGGGGGGGGG.

PRINCE JOHN. YOU LET THOSE FILTHY DISGUST-ING OUTLAWS DRAG OFF MY NEW WENCH IN THE FOREST WHILE YOU SCUTTLED SAFELY BACK TO NOTTINGHAM LIKE A PACK OF RAB-BITS? IS THAT AN ESCORT?

YORICK. *(Staggering around with the bag over his head, hic-cuping and choking.)* HIC. GGLLLGGLGLGLGLGGG. HIC. GGGLLGGGGG. HIC. HIC.

SHERIFF. We felt someone should return to report it, sire.

PRINCE JOHN. ALL OF YOU? YOU LEFT THAT SWEET, INNOCENT YOUNG TREMBLY FAWN-BREASTED VIRGIN WENCHY IN THE SLIMEY HANDS OF A DEPRAVED AND DEGRADED MISER-ABLE BUNCH OF MURDERERS IN THE DARK MID-DLE OF THE FOREST AND THEN YOU COME BACK HERE AND TELL ME YOU'VE GOT GOOD NEWS? DID YOU HEAR THAT, MOTHER? MOTHER?

QUEEN ELEANOR. *(asleep, snoring)* ZZZZZZZZZZZZZ-ZZZZZZZZZZZ.

PRINCE JOHN. *(snarling)* WAKE UP, MOTHER.

BRONWEN. Leave her be, she's a hundred and seven year old.

YORICK. HIC. HIC. HIC. GGGLGGGGLGGG.

SHERIFF. Well, it could be worse, sire.

PRINCE JOHN. WORSE? HOW COULD IT BE WORSE?

YORICK. *(Running back and forth hysterically with the bag over his head, having a massive hiccing and choking attack.)* HIC. HIC. HIC. HIC. GGGGGLLGGGGGGG. HICC.

SHERIFF. A bear might have eaten her.

PRINCE JOHN. A BEAR? A BEAR?

(He begins strangling the SHERIFF as SALLY returns balancing precariously an enormous tray of hot toddy in a silver tea service and YORICK'S attack moves to a climax.)

YORICK. HIC. HIC. HIC. HIC. HIC. *(SALLY is concentrating on keeping the tray, which is much too big for her, balanced properly, and YORICK, bag over his head and out of control, steps into her, knocking silver and toddy everywhere, mostly over SALLY.)*

SALLY. AAAAAAAAHHHHHHHHHHHHHHH.

YORICK. HIC. HIC. HIC. HIC. YYYGGGGRLRL-RLRLRLRLLGGGGGG. Ukkkkk. *(He clutches his throat and falls over, whack, very dramatic, bag still on his head.)*

SALLY. AAAAAAAAAAHHHHHHHHHHHHHH. *(The Sheriff, having his head beaten against a table, points frantically towards the jester in an effort to shift PRINCE JOHN'S attention. BRONWEN watches, a little bored, concerned with her feet. The Queen sleepeth. SALLY scrambles around desperately trying to gather up tea things and mop up with her dress. Finally PRINCE JOHN, who is tiring, looks where the SHERIFF is pointing.)*

PRINCE JOHN. All right, what is it? *(He sees YORICK*

spread-eagle on the floor, and SALLY sobbing and lifting the jester's leg to mop under it.) Hello. What's this? *(He drops the SHERIFF—thud—and investigates.)* I do believe old Yorick hath pulled the royal croak. Bloody hell. What a day. Sheriff?

SHERIFF. *(Cringing a bit in spite of himself.)* Yes sire?

PRINCE JOHN. I want every able-bodied person combing the forest for Maid Marian, and I want it posted, twenty-thousand pounds of the realm for Robin Hood's head, dead or alive, have you got that, Sheriff?

SHERIFF. Yes sire.

PRINCE JOHN. And order a new jester. This one's finally gone to Fool's Paradise.

SHERIFF. Yes sire.

PRINCE JOHN. And if I don't have Robin Hood's head on a platter by Tuesday next, I'll have yours instead.

SHERIFF. I'd be honored, sire. *(He schlumps out with some dignity.)*

PRINCE JOHN. And get rid of this body. *(The SHERIFF runs back in and slams directly into the back end of SALLY, who has just stood up with the full tray balanced carefully.)*

SALLY. AAAAHHHHHHHHHHHHHHHH. *(The tea service flies everywhere.)*

PRINCE JOHN. STOP THAT BLUBBERING.

SHERIFF. Yes sire.

PRINCE JOHN. Not you, HER. *(snarling into her face)* STOP THAT.

(She immediately shuts up and begins cleaning up in abject terror. The SHERIFF is dragging YORICK off by one arm and one leg. In the little silence here, the sound of the QUEEN'S snoring penetrates.)

QUEEN ELEANOR. ZZZZZZZZZZZZZZZZZZZZ.

PRINCE JOHN. *(kicking her chair)* WAKE UP, YOU FOUL-SMELLING, LECHEROUS OLD GORGON.

QUEEN ELEANOR. *(rousing)* What? Who? What is it?

PRINCE JOHN. I said, wake up, Mommy, it's time for your nap.

BRONWEN. You're a very tense person, you know that?

PRINCE JOHN. Tense? Me? Tense? I've got nerves of walnut. *(SALLY, about to make it offstage with the tray and what's left of the tea service, has been so busy looking back at PRINCE JOHN and trying to be cheery that she runs square into the wall. Crash.)* WILL YOU PEOPLE WATCH WHAT YOU'RE DOING? DOESN'T ANYBODY TEACH YOU PEOPLE HOW TO WALK?

SALLY. *(Running in several directions at once, falls down, gets up, runs out.)* AAAAAAAAAHHHHHHH. AAAAAA-HHHHHHH. AAAAAAHHHHHHH.

BRONWEN. You big bully.

PRINCE JOHN. Cretins. I am surrounded by cretins. *(He leans moodily upon a table, which falls over, sending him crashing to the floor. The QUEEN, who has been heading off to the john, stops and looks down at PRINCE JOHN there on the floor.)*

QUEEN ELEANOR. *(coldly)* Now THAT is funny. *(She walks out.)*

Scene 3

ROBIN'S camp in Sherwood Forest. The outlaws scattered about eating, sewing, whittling arrows, moving unobtrusively here and there as the scene progresses. MARIAN broods.

ALAN. *(singing)*
WITHIN THE FOREST DARK AND DEEP
AMONG THE GNARLED AND TWISTED WOODS
AMONG THE FALLEN CHERRY TREES
THE LADY SITS ALONE AND BROODS.
I WISH YOU WERE IN
THE WILD WOOD DEEP
I WISH YOU WERE IN THE SEA,
I WISH YOU WERE IN
THE BOTTOM OF HELL
AND FAR AWAY FROM ME
AND FAR AWAY FROM ME.

LITTLE JOHN. *(Coming over with DAVEY to where ROBIN and WILL SCARLET are eating.)* We got a problem with the young lady, Robin.

ROBIN. She demanding finger bowls and candles?

DAVEY. She won't eat nothin'. Not a bit. Won't touch it.

LITTLE JOHN. It ain't that I'm offended, exactly. I mean, taste is taste, and I ain't been to France to study cookin', I'm just scared she'll expire on us. Ladies is fragile.

WILL SCARLET. She don't look fragile to me, Johnny. That there is one powerful stubborn woman, quite a handful, and I'd give a good deal to have one or two hands full of her, tell you the truth.

DAVEY. Get her to eat somethin', Robin. We're worried about her.

ROBIN. All right. I'll give it a try.

WILL SCARLET. Watch out, Robin. Dangerous woman, that.

ROBIN. I'll be careful. *(He brings two plates of beans over to MARIAN, who sits ostentatiously pouting.)* Dinner is served, milady. *(She ignores him. He puts one plate down beside her and sits not too far away, eating.)* Not hungry this evening? *(no response)* Too ill to speak? My men are worried about you. They are, I swear. If you're not feeling well, we have a woman comes in with leeches, she can bleed you.

MARIAN. I am not ill. I do not converse with brigands.

ROBIN. Oh. Sorry.

MARIAN. What have you done with Lady Quigley?

ROBIN. I haven't done anything with her. She was having palpitations, I believe. Friar Tuck's looking after her.

MARIAN. Friar Tuck?

(QUIGLEY comes bursting through the camp screaming and giggling, pursued by FRIAR TUCK. They circumnavigate ROBIN and MARIAN.)

QUIGLEY. Woo HOOOOO. Oh, NOOOO. WOOOO. STOP. Hoo HOO. YOU DEVIL. WHOOOOAAA. HEEEEE HEE HEE. GET AWAY. HE HEE.

FRIAR TUCK. *(interspersed with the above)* HOO HOO HOO. GOTCHA GOTCHA GOTCHA. KOOTCHY KOOTCHY KOOTCHY. WHEEEEEEEE. *(They run back out again. MARIAN is indignant. ROBIN smiles and keeps eating.)*

ROBIN. She seems to be feeling better.

MARIAN. That revolting man is NOT a Friar.

ROBIN. He has many excellent qualities, one of which is tolerance for the frailties of others, a virtue which you, for one, seem a bit deficient in. And he IS a Friar, as far as I know. We're quite devout here, actually.

MARIAN. What do you worship? Trees?

ROBIN. I wouldn't speak ill of the trees, not here where they live. Our Lord was crucified upon a tree, and long before that the tree was a symbol connected with rebirth, resurrection, eternal life, and also with knowledge, as in the trees of life and knowledge in the garden of Eden, which this place much resembles. Friar Tuck says—

MARIAN. I do not dispute scripture with brigands. *(Pause. ROBIN looks at her.)*

ROBIN. Your supper's getting cold. Don't you eat with brigands, either?

MARIAN. I don't eat food stolen from the mouths of honest people.

ROBIN. My dear, you've been eating food stolen from honest people's mouths all your life.

MARIAN. I am NOT your dear, and I've never done any such thing.

ROBIN. What does your father do for a living?

MARIAN. You know perfectly well what he does. He's a gentleman, he doesn't do anything. What I mean is—

ROBIN. He's a landlord.

MARIAN. We have peasants living and working on our land, yes.

ROBIN. Do you pay many visits to the people who live on your father's land?

MARIAN. We pass by quite often, in our coach. They wave at us.

ROBIN. How many fingers do they hold up?

MARIAN. They look happy enough. Sometimes we stop.

ROBIN. But not too long, of course. You wouldn't want to get too close a look at them, would you?

MARIAN. Don't take that tone with me.

WILL STUTELY. *(With list and quill pen, he's been trying to get ROBIN'S attention.)* Pardon, Robin, but we have the inventory of what was taken from the Sheriff's party.

ROBIN. Good. What have we got?

WILL STUTELY. One case of French wine for Prince John, and some fresh peaches.

ROBIN. I think we can find some use for that.

WILL STUTELY. A strong box containing ninety-seven gold pieces, the rents from Doncaster.

ROBIN. We'll hang onto that, too, for right now.

MARIAN. Criminal. Thief. Hypocrite.

WILL STUTELY. One shipment of pickles and herring for Eadom at the Blue Boar Inn.

ROBIN. We'll deliver that tomorrow. Mind you keep Friar Tuck out of it.

WILL STUTELY. Can we deliver it tonight, Robin? It's smelling up the whole camp.

ROBIN. It'll be clear tonight. Full moon.

WILL STUTELY. We'd rather take the risk.

ROBIN. All right. What else?

WILL STUTELY. A trunk containing many dresses and items of personal ladies' apparel of an intimate nature—

MARIAN. My CLOTHES. IF YOU LAY SO MUCH AS

ONE FINGER UPON MY CLOTHING, YOU BAR-
BARIAN, I'LL—

WILL STUTELY. *(backing away)* I'm sorry miss, we
haven't harmed them, but we must take the inventory.

MARIAN. Just keep your filthy hands out of my
wardrobe.

WILL STUTELY. *(offended)* I washed my hands before I
ate my supper, miss. I hope you can say the same.

ROBIN. Cut the gowns up into squares.

WILL STUTELY. Righto. *(He goes off smiling.)*

MARIAN. Into squares? Cut my gowns up into squares?
You wouldn't DARE.

ROBIN. Yes I would.

MARIAN. You, OHHHHHH, you ANIMALS.

ROBIN. Now there you go again—first you're slander-
ing the trees and now the animals. You are in fact yourself
a kind of animal—the kind which has the power to
choose what kind of animal she is, though you abuse
the gift.

MARIAN. I don't know what you're talking about.

ROBIN. It's not a jackal's fault that he's a jackal, he's got
no choice, and so for him there's some dignity in being
simply what he is—but if a landlord, say, should choose
to do his business like a jackal, that's different.

MARIAN. You ARROGANT, CONTEMPTIBLE, HEART-
LESS, DESPICABLE—

ROBIN. You retreat into hysteria.

MARIAN. DON'T CALL ME HYSTERICAL. I'M NOT
HYSTERICAL, I'M FURIOUS.

ROBIN. Well, good, that's a start, anyway.

MARIAN. EITHER RELEASE US OR KILL US AND BE DONE WITH IT, I WILL NOT SIT BY AND WATCH MY BEAUTIFUL GOWNS CUT UP INTO SQUARES PURELY OUT OF SPITE.

ROBIN. Would you like to make a little trip with me tomorrow?

MARIAN. CERTAINLY NOT. Where?

ROBIN. To visit your father's estate.

MARIAN. You want to take me home?

ROBIN. I might, if you'll stop shrieking at me long enough to eat your supper.

MARIAN. I don't believe you. You're just trying to get me to shut up.

ROBIN. Yes, frankly, I would like you to shut up, I'd also like you to eat something, but I'm not lying. I'm attempting to strike a simple bargain, despite the fact that I rather guess bargaining is another of those numerous activities you do not engage in with brigands.

MARIAN. If I agree to be quiet—

ROBIN. And eat your supper.

MARIAN. And eat that loathesome mess there, you'll swear to take me to my father's estate tomorrow?

ROBIN. That's it.

MARIAN. How do I know I can trust you?

ROBIN. You don't. But if I'm lying, you'll find out soon enough, and then you can scream all you want and never trust a brigand again, all right?

MARIAN. I could be dead by tomorrow.

ROBIN. You might be if you don't eat.

MARIAN. What if I refuse?

ROBIN. Then I'll hog tie you, force feed you, place a

gag in your mouth and stuff you in a potato sack for the night. I will not have anybody going hungry in my camp, nor will I have a hyst—I mean, furious woman howling my whereabouts to half the population of England. So, are you going to be still and eat your supper, or not? *(She thinks about it, looks at her plate.)*

MARIAN. What is this? It looks dreadful.

ROBIN. It's beans. They're quite good

MARIAN. You eat beans? Aren't you poachers? Don't you eat venison?

ROBIN. Not often, no.

MARIAN. But they say you're the best archer in the kingdom.

ROBIN. Oh, I am, I just don't, to be perfectly honest, really enjoy killing very much. Try to keep it quiet, will you? It's bad for business.

MARIAN. You don't seem to mind killing the Sheriff's men.

ROBIN. Did you see me kill anyone?

MARIAN. Well, no, not actually, but—

ROBIN. Did you see any of my men kill anybody?

MARIAN. No, but everybody knows that—

ROBIN. I'm not responsible for the exaggerations of local romance. We'll bring down an old stag now and then if one of Prince John's sub-moronic hunters has left it wounded—they cry, you know. They have great brown sad eyes and they cry real tears when they're hurt. The deer, not the hunters.

MARIAN. Do you expect me to believe you never killed anybody?

ROBIN. I didn't say that.

MARIAN. Then you admit you're a murderer.

ROBIN. If you must know, I killed my father, I believe that qualifies me, I just don't run about the countryside making a habit of it. Does that satisfy you? *(MARIAN looks at him, not sure what to say.)* If you don't at least pretend to like those beans, you're going to break Little John's heart.

MARIAN. Oh, all right. *(She begins to eat, reluctantly at first, but with increasingly ill-concealed voracity.)*

ROBIN. That's not so bad, is it?

MARIAN. *(mouth full)* It's perfectly horrid. *(ROBIN gives the thumbs up sign to the outlaws, who begin to cheer, clap and whistle.)*

MERRY MEN. YAAAAAYYYYYYYYY.

MARIAN. Why are they doing that? Why are they looking at me?

ROBIN. They've never seen a lady eat. All right, men, back to work, come on, don't gape. Well, you go on and eat, I have a little journey to make before I sleep tonight.

MARIAN. You're not leaving me alone here, are you?

ROBIN. I'll leave Friar Tuck to watch over you. And one or two others to watch over HIM. You'll be quite safe.

MARIAN. You're really taking me home tomorrow?

ROBIN. Get a good night's rest, you'll need it. There's more in the pot. Courage. *(He goes. She looks after him, eating, troubled.)*

ALAN. *(singing)*
THE MOON ROSE UP
AND THE WOOD WAS FULL

OF SHADOW THINGS COME OUT TO PLAY
AND WHILE SHE LAY
STARING AT THE SKY
HER LOVER CREPT FAR AWAY, MY LOVE,
HER LOVER CREPT FAR AWAY.

Scene 4

Night at the Blue Boar Inn. ELLEN and JENNY are cleaning up.
COOTIE THE DRUNK, with his head lying on a table,
and CRAZY BETTY, the old witchy woman, laying out
tarot cards. ELLEN and JENNY are used to both and work
around them.

ELLEN. It's true, Jenny, I seen the men with axes, they
be cuttin' down the whole forest soon.

JENNY. Where I was born there was a lovely forest
once, and now it's all bogs and sump holes. You think it
can't go away until it's gone, and then what's to
replace it?

ELLEN. A tennis court, I heard.

JENNY. What manner of thing is that?

ELLEN. I don't know, but it can't be anything Chris-
tian, for I hear that gentlemen go there to swear at each
other. The whole kingdom's fell apart with good King
Richard Lion Heart held ransom off in Austria.

JENNY. They say he must be dead.

ELLEN. I don't believe it. Cootie, move yer feet. I be

cleanin' there, and we got to close.

COOTIE THE DRUNK. Farfalafalarfl um.

ELLEN. You're welcome.

JENNY. Poor Cootie, since they took his land away he ain't been worth his own spit. Sometimes it makes me so mad I—

ELLEN. Listen. Did you hear that noise?

JENNY. What kind of noise?

CRAZY BETTY. Tis some cold dead thing in the night.

ELLEN. Jenny, where do you think the thing will go when they've cut the forest down, the dark thing lives in the woods that trails about and moans at night and makes the piping sound?

JENNY. I don't want to talk about no thing.

CRAZY BETTY. Cold dead slimey thing in the woods.

JENNY. You stop it, now, Crazy Betty.

ELLEN. It's real, Jenny, I seen it once, stayed too late at Gummy Granny's, come home through the woods and heard the thing behind me, it was like a piece of wind at first, bit of cool somethin' up the back of me dress, then a small whistly sound like pipes. They say—

JENNY. I don't want to hear what they say. I've just last week got rid of me fear of what's under the bed.

ELLEN. They say the thing is Death, waits in the woods, and when it's your time he lures you to the forest on some common errand, and then he takes you.

JENNY. Stop it, Ellen, you're scarin' me, now.

(EADOM comes out from the back, with an apron.)

EADOM. Are you two paid to work or paid to jabber?

ELLEN. We're seldom paid at all.

EADOM. Yer paid more than yer worth. My dead wife used to say, each time she would empty the chamber pot—

ELLEN. Did you hear it then?

JENNY. I heard it too, that time. A kind of piping sound from the woods.

CRAZY BETTY. Bad thing comin' this way. I turned up the Death card.

EADOM. AAAAWW, anythin' to keep from workin'. You girls be about as much good to me as a violin to a pig. I've half a—

(The sound, clear now, they all hear it, a very eerie piping sound.)

JENNY. *(clutching onto ELLEN)* Oh my, oh my, oh my.

CRAZY BETTY. Gettin' closer. Slatherin' through the woods to us, twill be knockin' on the door soon.

EADOM. I don't hear nothin', exactly, but I think I'll bar the door, just to reassure you wimmin.

(He moves to the door but just then comes a heavy knock, three times, loud and ominous, that freezes him in his tracks.)

ELLEN. Don't answer it.

EADOM. Do you think I'm afraid of a knock on me own door?

CRAZY BETTY. Go to the door the blind man said and let death in.

EADOM. Jenny, you open it.

ELLEN. Eadom, you great coward, shame on you.
EADOM. You're so brave, YOU open it.
ELLEN. All right. I will.

(She moves to the door and the knock comes agagin, three times, louder. ELLEN jumps back. Pause.)

COOTIE THE DRUNK. *(Raising his head. Loud.)* Come in.

(He drops his head again. They rush to shut him up, but it's too late. The door creaks open, revealing an ominous looking figure, hooded, with black gloves on long twisted hands. They stare at him. Pause.)

ELLEN. Is there something you be wanting, sir?

DARK MONK. *(Polite, mocking, charming, unpleasant.)* Is there something I be wanting? Yes. Yes, there is. Where is the one they call Robin Hood?

ELLEN. He's not here.

DARK MONK. I can see he is not here. Where can I find him?

ELLEN. Who be askin' for Robin Hood, if I may enquire?

DARK MONK. One who has private business with him.

EADOM. We don't know.

DARK MONK. *(level, threatening)* I think you will tell me, and now. *(pause)*

EADOM. He may be headin' up to North Barnstaple.
ELLEN. EADOM.

EADOM. He may be, I say. And maybe not.

ELLEN. Just what is your business with him, sir?

DARK MONK. I would not be anxious to pry too deeply into the darker crevices of why and wherefore, my dear. There are things you think you want to know that you in fact perhaps do not. Treasure your ignorance, it's all you get to keep. I thank you for your kindness, and hope to see you soon again. I'm drawn especially to the young, they have such tender flesh. Good night, my friends. *(He goes. They stare at the doorway.)*

COOTIE THE DRUNK. GNIGHT. *(EADOM closes the door and bolts it.)*

ELLEN. You shouldna told him where Robin was.

EADOM. He's only one old monk, I hardly think he's any harm.

ELLEN. Then why are you shaking like that?

CRAZY BETTY. Can you smell the death? There was death in this place. *(COOTIE smells his armpit.)*

ELLEN. Someone must go and warn them. I'm sorry, Jenny, to put all the work on you, but I must go tell Robin.

CRAZY BETTY. I'd not go out tonight.

ELLEN. *(Putting on her wrap and starting out.)* I don't like that thing, whatever it was, and I must—

(Looking back to talk, she's run into an enormous hooded figure.)

ELLEN. AAAAHHHHHHHHHH. *(The thing holds ELLEN. EADOM hides under the table and COOTIE joins him to avoid the screaming.)*

JENNY. *(Rushing at the figure and whacking at it with the broom.)* YOU LET HER GO, YOU BEAST, YOU FILTHY DEVIL THING.

LITTLE JOHN. *(Putting down his hood.)* Jenny Brown, do you mean to kill me with the broom?

ELLEN. It's Little John. Oh, never was I so glad to see such an ugly man. *(She and JENNY hug him.)*

LITTLE JOHN. What's the matter with you folk? Seen a ghostie?

ELLEN. I think we have.

(ROBIN comes in with WILL SCARLET.)

ROBIN. Here, what's all the screaming?

ELLEN. There was a Dark Monk from the woods, Robin, and he asked for you, and yonder great idiot told him you were going north tomorrow.

EADOM. I said perhaps, to throw him off.

ROBIN. It's all right. You did no harm.

JENNY. He said he had private business with you.

ROBIN. Then he shall find me, by and by.

JENNY. Do you think it's the creature in the stories, that comes to you when you're about to— *(She stops, realizing what she's saying.)*

ROBIN. More likely it's a poor monk in need of money.

ELLEN. No, Robin, I smelled a darker purpose there, he frightened us. You'd best stay home tomorrow.

ROBIN. I've folk expecting me, and now I've promised someone I'd take her home. It's not my time to die yet, is it, Betty?

CRAZY BETTY. Old Betty read the cards for ye when you was a boy, and they said you'd either die a young man or live forever.

ROBIN. And as the latter seems unlikely, I've always presumed the former, if one's to believe you, Betty.

CRAZY BETTY. I did predict your father's death, and other things.

ROBIN. Indeed you did. It's not a thing I choose to worry over, though. Now don't all look so glum. Ellen, your lover Alan's in the back, cursing the pickled herring, and Davey's there, too, Jenny, go and see them now, but don't get too close, they smell like a fish market. Go on. *(ELLEN and JENNY go out, still troubled.)*

EADOM. I'm sorry, Robin, about the monk. The fact is, I'm a coward.

ROBIN. *(Putting his arm around him.)* Then you and I are brothers, for I have always been one, too. I'll tell no one if you won't. Fair enough?

EADOM. Thank you. I've got to count me fish. *(He goes out. ROBIN sees LITTLE JOHN and WILL SCARLET looking worried.)*

ROBIN. Don't look at me like that. I see no harm a monk can do. I won't change my plans for him.

CRAZY BETTY. When a man's time to die has come, the pipe sounds in the wildwood.

ROBIN. Well, I hope it isn't mine, I've many things to do yet. Now, we'd best get back, I don't want to leave that girl alone with Friar Tuck too long.

WILL SCARLET. Will Stutely's there to mind her. Do I detect that Robin likes the lady somewhat?

ROBIN. Too rich for me. And got too much to learn.

WILL SCARLET. So do we all.

ROBIN. So do we all, that's true. One drink with these good folk, just one, and then we're off.

WILL SCARLET. One drink.

LITTLE JOHN. One drink. *(WILL and ROBIN go out. LITTLE JOHN is following but spies a half-full glass of beer on the table beneath which COOTIE lies.)* Maybe a drink and a half. *(He goes over to finish the beer.)* I ain't feared o' none o' yer spooks, Betty. *(COOTIE. roused from slumber, reaches out and grabs LITTLE JOHN'S leg.)* AAAAAAAAHHHHH-HHHHHHHH. *(He falls over the chair and starts to crawl away in terror, then sees who it is, as CRAZY BETTY cackles happily.)* COOTIE, YOU SLUG, YOU SCARED THE BEJESUS OUT OF ME.

WILL SCARLET. *(rushing back in)* What is it now?

LITTLE JOHN. Cootie and me was just foolin' a bit, playin' spooks. Come on. One drink. Don't you be sneakin' nothin' on me. *(He goes out. WILL follows.)*

COOTIE THE DRUNK. Was somebody just here?

CRAZY BETTY. Just a dead man and his friends. That's all it was.

ALAN. *(sings)*
I MET A DEAD MAN IN THE WOOD
I MET THE DEVIL ON THE HILL
I MET MY TRUE LOVE COLD AND WHITE
UPON HER LIPS IT WAS SO CHILL.

Scene 5

Roosterscrow. Birds sing. Morning in the forest. TUCK drinks with QUIGLEY, who wears a Merry Man hat with a false arrow through her head.

QUIGLEY. *(Laughing her high-pitched, drunken and rather wicked laugh.)* Oh, Friar Tuck, you're a wicked fellow, a wicked fellow indeedy, you make me blush inside.

FRIAR TUCK. Wicked? Be I wicked? Eftsoons, Madame, alack, I do what I do but for the greater Glory of God, as an example and warning to others.

QUIGLEY. An example to others? I came to you believing I was about to be murdered by cutthroat robbers, to confess my sins like a good woman, and in one night with you I have managed to commit sins I had never even suspected to exist.

FRIAR TUCK. I am but teaching you, madame, the seventeen deadly sins, and how evil they be. We have simply moved through them, one by one. It is all part of your religious education.

QUIGLEY. Well, you're a wonderful teacher, and I've certainly learned a great deal, but, Friar, you know, I do swear, this night of drinking sack and eating beans has filled my poor stomach with the most noxious and discomfortable gases I have yet experienced. I feel, and am, as twere, all impregnated with gaseosity.

FRIAR TUCK. Ah, Lady Quigley, that is because I have

43

yet one more lesson to teach thee, and this is the most pleasurable of all, which cometh after one hath committed successfully in turn and renounced forever all the other deadly sins.

QUIGLEY. Oh, my. And what might that be?

FRIAR TUCK. Be a good student, Lady Quigley, and I shall now teach thee how to fart.

QUIGLEY. To fart?

FRIAR TUCK. One thing a holy person like myself does learn, madame, in the course of his multitudinous studies, is that there is no greater pleasure in this world, my dear, than a good, strong farting in the morning.

QUIGLEY. But sir, is this a thing a lady doeth?

FRIAR TUCK. Of course, madame. All the great women of history have been prodigious farters. Helen of Troy, says Homer, did lay a fart so loud, a part of the walls of the city did crumble, allowing the Greeks to enter. Cleopatra was well known by Plutarch and others to have propelled her barge along the Nile on many occasions by the judicious application of a well-timed, well-placed fart or two. And Sappho, the great poetress, has left us the renowned fragment which, roughly translated by the Venerable Bede, doth run:
I do declare there is some art
in making you a perfect fart.
It is no easy matter, mum,
to push this air out from my bum
in such a way that I may pass
enchanting music through—

(*MARIAN, stomping in, interrupting, furious, wearing only a quilt.*)

MARIAN. LADY QUIGLEY. Where on EARTH have you BEEN? Do you think to abandon me? Has thou spent the whole night drinking and fornicating in the forest with this person?

QUIGLEY. Certainly not. A part of the time I spent drinking and fornicating with some of the others. Hic.

MARIAN. Where is my gown? I left it on the rocks while I was bathing in the brook, and when I returned, there was this smelly old quilt left in its place.

QUIGLEY. Clearly your gown hath been abducted.

MARIAN. By whom? And for what purpose? Am I to be ravished after all?

QUIGLEY. I don't know, maybe the Merry Men like to dress up in them. *(She laughs her high pitched laugh.)* Maybe that's what makes them so Merry. *(again the laugh)*

MARIAN. You are intoxicated, and I am ashamed for you.

QUIGLEY. Well, you talk awful high and mighty for a lady wearin' a old barn quilt. I'd rather be a drunk old hag than a prissy little ice cube virgin with her nose up in the air like the end part of a chicken. *(The high pitched laugh, which is beginning to hurt FRIAR TUCK'S ears.)*

MARIAN. I can't believe you're speaking to me this way. What has this man done to you?

QUIGLEY. Not half as much as I'd like him to. *(The laugh again. FRIAR TUCK anticipates this one and has his hands over his ears.)* Oh, if you want a dress so bad, you can have mine. Here, just let me get these damn snapples loose. Why do they rope us in like we was under arrest, when all they can think about is gettin' us naked? Here, Friar, just pull on that. No, not that, THAT. You can pull on THAT later. *(She is trying to get her dress over her head.)*

MARIAN. Lady Quigley, stop that, stop it.

FRIAR TUCK. No, go ahead. It's all right, miss, I've seen it. *(The MERRY MEN have begun to stop and watch.)*

(ROBIN enters.)

ROBIN. You promised you'd be quiet.

MARIAN. Where is my gown?

ROBIN. *(Holding out a wretched, raggedy dress.)* Here it is.

MARIAN. That's not my gown. That looks like something you'd wipe a privy with.

ROBIN. That was last week. Now it's for you. If you want to visit your father today.

MARIAN. I will not let that foul thing touch my body.

ROBIN. Well, I can't be dragging you about the countryside in what you usually wear, it might tend to draw attention, us dressed like simple outlaws and you like the Queen of Clubs.

MARIAN. *(Folding her arms and stomping.)* I won't wear that.

ROBIN. Then you'll come naked.

MARIAN. I CERTAINLY WILL NOT COME NAKED. *(She stomps, hurts her foot, nearly loses the quilt. The MERRY MEN are all watching.)*

WILL SCARLET. How many vote she wears the dress?

MERRY MEN. NAY. BOOOOO. NOO.

WILL SCARLET. How many vote for naked?

MERRY MEN. *(clapping and cheering)* YAYYYYYY. WE

WANT NAKED. YAYYYYY.

WILL SCARLET. I'm afraid the nakeds have it.

ROBIN. Your opinion is duly noted, now go about your business.

DAVEY. We was just bein' democratic. *(They scatter.)*

MARIAN. I want my gown back, and I want it now.

ROBIN. You can't have it.

MARIAN. It's certainly going to call some attention to us also if I go naked, is it not?

ROBIN. Yes, but it might be worth the risk. In any case, your gown's been cut up into squares.

MARIAN. Oh, no.

ROBIN. I'm afraid so.

MARIAN. I'm going to enjoy it when they draw and quarter you.

ROBIN. Either you wear this, or you go in the suit you were born in, or you don't go at all, I haven't time to argue with you. Do you want to see Daddy or not?

MARIAN. *(Hesitating, then snatching up the ragged dress and going behind a tree to put it on.)* You'll regret this, mark my words, you WILL regret it.

ROBIN. I have no doubt.

FRIAR TUCK. That's the way, Robin, take a firm hand.

ROBIN. And you two get sobered up—I'll have no drunks in my camp.

FRIAR TUCK. You're a testy one today. Cupid's little arrows strike the great Robin Hood where he liveth. As the beloved Saint Thomas Aquinas once said to his horse—

ROBIN. What on earth is that awful smell?

FRIAR TUCK. Don't look at me, I was just giving Quigley her catechism.

ROBIN. Must be those polecats again. We may have to move camp. Lord, what a stench. *(He goes out.)*

FRIAR TUCK. *(looking at QUIGLEY)* That was very good.

QUIGLEY. I thought it was you.

FRIAR TUCK. No, twasn't me, I keep track.

QUIGLEY. You count them? Whatever for?

FRIAR TUCK. *(as they go off discussing this)* Oh, I don't know, it helps pass the time. Are you sure it wasn't you?

QUIGLEY. *(disappearing)* I don't think it was. *(They go off discussing this.)*

ALAN. *(singing)*

WHAT WILL YOU LEAVE TO YOUR BROTHER JOHN?

THE GALLOWS TREE TO HANG HIM ON.

WHAT WILL YOU LEAVE TO YOUR BROTHER'S WIFE?

THE WILDERNESS TO END HER LIFE.

WHAT WILL YOU LEAVE TO THE WOODS SO GRAND?

I WILL MAKE IT INTO A DESERT LAND.

Scene 6

Nottingham castle. PRINCE JOHN looking at a great map

unrolled on a table, the sides of which keep rolling up on him.
BRONWEN looks over his shoulder, eating a peach noisily.
The QUEEN sleeps sitting up. GILL REDCAP at attention
beside her. Each time she begins to lean sideways in her
sleep, he pushes her back to a straight up position. This hap-
pens now and then through the scene.

PRINCE JOHN. Will you stop gawking over my shoulder? Your peach drippeth upon my neck.

BRONWEN. Building another great stupid castle, are you?

PRINCE JOHN. This is the plan for the tennis court in Sherwood Forest.

BRONWEN. Ain't it hard to play tennis with all them trees in the way?

PRINCE JOHN. We're going to cut down all the trees. There's a wood shortage in the Low Countries. We'll make a killing.

BRONWEN. But what's a forest without trees?

PRINCE JOHN. A tennis court.

BRONWEN. You don't need to cut down a whole bloody forest just to build a tennis court.

PRINCE JOHN. No, there'll also be a golfing course, a sword and spear manufactory, a debtors prison, several slaughterhouses—

BRONWEN. Won't that stink up the tennis?

PRINCE JOHN. It's an immense forest, Bronwen, there's plenty of room for everything.

BRONWEN. Except the trees. And the squirrels.

PRINCE JOHN. We can't stop the forward movement of Western civilization for a few squirrels.

BRONWEN. I would. I like squirrels. Used to have a pet squirrel, slept with me and everything. Alfred, his name was. Probably got relatives there.

PRINCE JOHN. There will always be squirrels, as long as there are nuts.

BRONWEN. Won't be no nuts if there ain't no trees.

PRINCE JOHN. Squirrels find nuts.

BRONWEN. Well, I don't like it.

PRINCE JOHN. I don't CARE.

BRONWEN. And we don't need no debtors prisons, you shouldn't put folk in jail for bein' poor.

PRINCE JOHN. The poor like jail. Look how many of them we've got in there already. How many rich people have you seen in jail? Now be quiet and let me work.

BRONWEN. You going to marry this Maid Marian if they get her back?

PRINCE JOHN. Good God, no, whatever gave you that idea?

BRONWEN. It ain't right to lure innocent women thinkin' you're going to marry them.

PRINCE JOHN. You're hardly qualified to speak about innocence.

BRONWEN. I was innocent once. I must have been.

PRINCE JOHN. Just watch out, or you'll find yourself back in Wales, slopping the pigs.

BRONWEN. I wouldn't half mind. Like to see Alfred again. He could show me his nuts.

PRINCE JOHN. That's charming.

(GROK leaps in and doing a somersault which is so reckless it is rather alarming—it is also rather badly done. GROK'S trademark

*being that although he throws himself about with great confidence,
he is seldom far from disaster.)*

GROK. DA DAAAAAAAAAAAAAHHHHHHHHHH.

PRINCE JOHN. *(Greatly startled, getting tangled in the map.)*
What the hell is that?

(The SHERIFF comes in behind GROK.)

SHERIFF. It's the new jester, sire. Grok the Magni-
ficent.

PRINCE JOHN. Oh. Well, at least you've found a
younger one.

GROK. *(doing an elaborate obeisance)* Gaflooty.

PRINCE JOHN. Pardon?

GROK. *(spotting BRONWEN)* Yspricky! Yasphrutty!
Ooooo. Gazoobas. Hey. Yonka, yonka! *(He honks his horn
twice and bursts out laughing.)*

PRINCE JOHN. *(Wanting to be amused, but a little uncertain.)*
What did he say?

GROK. Wicknooty?

SHERIFF. I don't know, sire, I don't speak his language.

GROK. *(Making some sort of jest in the direction of BRON-
WEN'S chest area.)* Klisnootski fyorbin RUCKLE FARKEL
PUCK! HEY! *(On HEY he gets down on one knee and holds
arms out wide, waiting for applause.)*

PRINCE JOHN. *(staring at him)* What?

GROK. Huckle buckle? Yorny yorny?

PRINCE JOHN. *(to BRONWEN)* Is this Welsh?

BRONWEN. I hope not.

PRINCE JOHN. Doesn't this man speak English?

SHERIFF. Not yet.

PRINCE JOHN. Not yet? What am I supposed to do? teach him?

SHERIFF. We thought he might pick it up as he went along.

PRINCE JOHN. Here I am, at the head of the greatest kingdom in all of Christendom, while my brother rots in Austria and my mother's mind disintegrates, and I can't get a jester under ninety-seven who speaks a language I can understand?

GROK. Bobbo bullibniok shlubski fiziak! Skobby skobby doo waa, HEY? Ya?

PRINCE JOHN. *(deciding to ignore this)* What about Maid Marian? Have you found her?

SHERIFF. Not exactly, sire.

PRINCE JOHN. What do you mean, not exactly? Either you've found her or you haven't.

SHERIFF. We found part of her, sire. I mean, we found her shoe.

PRINCE JOHN. Aha. Now we're getting somewhere. And just where did you find her shoe? Not on her foot, I hope.

SHERIFF. In the forest, sire, where the outlaws surprised us.

PRINCE JOHN. And how does that help us?

SHERIFF. It tells us, sire, to look for a woman with one bare foot.

GROK. *(standing on his head)* NYUCKO SPIKORBY HERPY WHEEUP! WHUPP! WHUPP!

PRINCE JOHN. Where did we get this person, anyway?

Where's he from? Can we get rid of him? He's getting on my nerves.

SHERIFF. We tried getting rid of him earlier, sire, but he keeps coming back. We thought we might as well let you have a look at him, on the off chance you might LIKE that sort of thing.

GROK. *(Doing a little insane dance in a circle on one leg with his thumb in his ear, smiling.)* YESTROY YECKO BLO-ORA! HEY!

PRINCE JOHN. I find it hard to believe there is anyplace on earth where anybody however stupid likes THAT sort of thing.

GROK. WHOODY WHOODY WHOODY! WHO-ODY HEY! HEY HEY! *(Each time he says HEY, he faces the PRINCE on one knee, arms held out wide, smiling broadly.)*

BRONWEN. Eee's havin' a bloody fit.

SHERIFF. Maybe we could get him a translator.

PRINCE JOHN. I don't think I want to know what it means. It can't be anything good.

SHERIFF. Shall we have him killed, sire?

PRINCE JOHN. I'm surprised someone hasn't done that already. His mother, say.

GROK. *(Dancing in a circle, grinning and making bizarre faces.)* YOCKA HUCKLA HUCKLE BUCKA HUCKLE BUCKA HEY!

PRINCE JOHN. Listen, all right, Grok, that's enough of that, you can go, you are dismissed, please leave—

GROK. *(smiling and nodding)* Yorky ycklien DDDo-ooDAAAA. DDDooooDAA. Fronkiy finkola spooby dorg dorg dorg dag buvvuh wikky UP YUP—

PRINCE JOHN. WILL YOU SHUT UP!

GROK. *(Reacting as if this were an English ritual of friendship, mirroring him.)* VILLL HYOOOOOOOO SHATTTO-PPPPP.

PRINCE JOHN. SHADDDUPPPPP.

GROK. SHATTTOPPPPPPP.

PRINCE JOHN. SHADDDUPPPPPP.

GROK. SHADDDOOOOOOOPPPP. *(PRINCE JOHN smashes GROK over the head with a wine bottle.)* Oooooh, wucka ducka. *(GROK collapses in a heap.)*

BRONWEN. That wasn't very nice.

PRINCE JOHN. *(breathing hard)* Now you listen to me, Sheriff. I want Maid Marian, and I want her NOW, and I want the reward on Robin Head's hood—

SHERIFF. Robin Hood's head.

PRINCE JOHN. I want it doubled. No, tripled. Quadruple it. And I want those woods cleared of outlaws so we can start mowing down the trees. And I want to see that criminal's vital organs floating in my soup tureen. If it's not his, it's going to be yours, have you got that, Sheriff?

SHERIFF. I've got it.

PRINCE JOHN. Well, don't forget it. *(He steps on the recumbent GROK as he leaves.)*

GROK. Urk. Oh, yuckle.

BRONWEN. *(concerned for GROK)* Oh, poor baby, are you all right?

SHERIFF. Redcap, you come with me.

REDCAP. Yes sir. *(He goes off with the SHERIFF.)*

BRONWEN. We sure go through a lot of these. *(She lifts up GROK'S arm, lets go, it drops back, thud. The QUEEN veers to one side in her sleep, but now there is nobody to catch her, and she falls over on her head into the wastebasket.)*

Scene 7

A hovel on SIR STEPHEN'S estate.

ALAN. *(singing)*
MY FATHER HE HAD AN ACRE OF LAND
DOWN BY THE OCEAN SEA
HE SOWED IT WITH BONES
AND WATERED WITH BLOOD
ALL UNBEKNOWNST TO ME
ALL UNBEKNOWNST TO ME.

(Sounds of pigs. ROBIN pulls MARIAN in by the elbow.)

MARIAN. Liar. You said you'd bring me home. You've brought me to a pig sty.

ROBIN. It's on your father's estate, and you be civil, now, there's people live here.

MARIAN. Nobody would live here. And it's just as well, I couldn't bear for anybody to see me dressed in this filthy thing.

ROBIN. You're lovely, now control yourself, our hosts are here.

(GWENNY, a small pale girl of fifteen or thirty has appeared, in rags.)

ROBIN. Hello Gwenny.

GWENNY. Hlo, Robin.

ROBIN. It's all right, don't be afraid, it's just me.

GWENNY. Not afraid of you, Robin, mafeared of the lady a little.

ROBIN. What makes you think she's a lady?

GWENNY. Oh, she smells like a lady.

ROBIN. Does she? *(He sniffs at MARIAN and gets slapped at.)* She won't bite you, Gwenny, she only bites ME. Come here, she wants to meet you. Come on, we're better friends than that.

GWENNY. I put on me best dress when I heard you was comin', Robin, but I see she got a nicer one.

ROBIN. This is my friend Marian, Gwenny.

GWENNY. Pleased to meet you. Sir Stephen's daughter's called Marian, too.

ROBIN. Is she? And have you ever seen Sir Stephen's daughter?

GWENNY. Only from afar. The master never lets her out by where the pigs is, but I clumb a tree once, and saw her ridin' a white horse, and she looked so beatuiful, in her white dress, with her long hair trailin' behind her, and so far away. I dream about it sometimes.

ROBIN. Marian wants to know how you like living here on Sir Stephen's estate.

GWENNY. I don't know. Never lived noplace else. Just here with the pigs. It's all right, I guess.

ROBIN. Do you get enough to eat?

GWENNY. When you come by. We grow lots of food, but most goes for the rent, to Sir Stephen, and the tax to Prince John. And we got to save some for the pigs.

(ROBIN looks at MARIAN.)

MARIAN. Everybody pays taxes.

ROBIN. Does your father pay taxes?

MARIAN. Uh, I've never actually SEEN him pay taxes, but—

(OLD GUMMY GRANNY wanders in.)

OLD GUMMY GRANNY. Whoodle. Wheresa quilty, deary?

GWENNY. You got it in yer hand, Granny.

OLD GUMMY GRANNY. Oh? Do I? Well, a whoodle me arse.

GWENNY. This be Old Gummy Granny, miss. The quiltin' squares is lovely you brought us, Robin, they're the finest we ever had, so many pretty colors. That'll keep Granny warm another winter.

ROBIN. Those particular quilting squares are from Marian, here, it's her you should thank.

GWENNY. They're very fine, miss, thank you.

OLD GUMMY GRANNY. *(Holding up squares of cloth which look much like the gown MARIAN wore earlier.)* Nice quilties, yesss, oh yess, awhoodly fine uns.

GWENNY. Granny's our best quilter, though she's nearly forty.

MARIAN. She's forty? Gwenny, if you have so little to eat, why don't you ask Sir Stephen to help you?

GWENNY. Sir Stephen? Help us? He don't care a pig's pizzle what happens to us. When my Uncle Diccon went to ask a penny raise to feed the baby cause me sister died, Sir Stephen had him flogged for botherin' him.

MARIAN. Oh, I can't believe that's true.

GWENNY. Twas me that had to clean his back, and a mess it was, looked like when the hay bale fell on Fred the chicken. Baby better off in heaven, anyways. Little fingers and toes she had. Little sad eyes.

MARIAN. Maybe Sir Stephen's daughter could help you.

GWENNY. Oh, she ain't got time for us, she don't even know we exist. Not that I'm criticizin'. I wish I was her. You'll have to excuse me, I got to go feed Granny and shoe the horses.

MARIAN. You shoe the horses?

GWENNY. Ain't no young men to do it, just outlaws, all the rest been took into the army, sent to the Low Countries or someplace. Me brother Jack I ain't heard from since I was seven, he can't write and I can't read, but it's all right, some things don't bear much lookin' into, as the old lady said in the outhouse. Eat with us, Robin, beans today, special for you. Get a move on, Granny, don't drool on the nice lady.

OLD GUMMY GRANNY. Whoodle me quiltie, whoodle, whoodle. *(They go out. ROBIN looks at MARIAN.)*

MARIAN. Well, why do you cut the gowns into squares? Why not just give them the gowns whole?

ROBIN. Be a fine thing if your father saw his peasants wearing your gowns to slop the pigs, wouldn't it?

MARIAN. Then why not sell the gowns and give them the money?

ROBIN. They don't want charity. They give us some of the quilts they make and we sell them and split the profit. We're partners.

MARIAN. If my father really knew his tenants were living

like this—

ROBIN. He knows. He doesn't care.

MARIAN. My father is a good man, and I won't have you insulting him.

ROBIN. I'm not insulting anybody, I'm stating a fact. To you, he's been a good, kind, bumbling old hero, of that I have no doubt. To these people he is something quite different. It depends a good deal on where you're looking at him from, and how full your stomach is.

(FLINT comes sailing in on a board with wheels and a flurry of rags, legless.)

FLINT. WHEEEEEEEEEEEEEEEEEEEEEEE. *(He grabs MARIAN and wheels round to a stop.)* WHOOOO. Pardon, miss, just had me wheels greased, howdy doody. Davey says you want to see me, Robin.

ROBIN. Flint, would you tell my friend the story of how you lost your legs?

FLINT. Oh, that's a good one. I was drafted, miss, into his majesty's wars in the Great Netherland Swamps, and fought for my country three years. One leg was shot to hell, the other wasn't, but the barber what surgeoned me had too much to drink, been awake six days off and on, and he was eighty or ninety and had but one eye, and he'd got so much blood on the second leg from the first that he forgot which was which, so he took 'em both off, so as not to make a mistake. Robin found me beggin' in London and brought me back home—I used to load hay up at Sir Stephen's barns when I had legs. You know, miss, you look a bit like his little girl. 'Course, I ain't seen her in a long time.

MARIAN. You're Flint, that used to dance with the milkmaids.

FLINT. Yes, there's many come to see me dance in them days. My dancin' has degenerated somewhat since.

MARIAN. Flint, Sir Stephen doesn't know about your troubles, does he?

FLINT. Oh, yes, I went to speak to him when I first come back, just wheeled myself up the road, but it didn't do much good.

MARIAN. Perhaps he didn't recognize you.

FLINT. No, he knew me, for he called out my name, he said, Flint, get out of the road, and then he run over me with his horse. Still got the hoof marks on me chest, hurts when it rains.

MARIAN. That's horrible.

FLINT. Oh, I dunno. Twas his road. Excuse me, miss, I got a drinkin' and singin' contest with Friar Tuck—there's always good times when Robin comes. You sure do put me in mind of Sir Stephen's girl. She was always fond of me, would sit in my lap, when I had a lap.

(FRIAR TUCK comes on shouting.)

FRIAR TUCK. COME ON, FLINT, YOU SHORT SON OF A SLUT, I'VE ALREADY DRANK YOU UNDER THE TABLE AND YOU AIN'T EVEN STARTED YET. STOP BOTHERIN' ROBIN, CAN'T YOU SEE THE MAN'S IN LOVE?

FLINT. ALL RIGHT, YE GREAT SLOBBERY WHALE,

I'M COMIN'. *(He grabs onto the FRIAR'S habit and gets a free ride off, singing.)*
BUT THE SWEETEST ROSE MY LADY HAS
IS THE ROSE I CANNOT TOUCH—

FLINT and FRIAR TUCK. *(Singing as they disappear.)*
THOUGH I'D LIKE TO VERY MUCH.
(ROBIN looks at MARIAN.)

MARIAN. Look, if you let me go, I'll tell my father about this and I know he'll do something.

ROBIN. No he won't.

MARIAN. Will you at least let me go and try? He'll pay your ranson, if that's what you're worried about.

ROBIN. Your father's house is over that way.

MARIAN. I know where it is. You're really going to release me?

ROBIN. I said I would.

MARIAN. What about Lady Quigley?

ROBIN. She can go any time she pleases, although I suspect it's not going to be easy getting rid of her.

MARIAN. All right. What's your ransom price?

ROBIN. I don't believe in hostages. That's the sort of thing Prince John would do. We don't do that.

MARIAN. Why not? It would seem a very practical strategy to me.

ROBIN. I'm sure it would. That's how your side thinks. But I'm not on your side. The worst thing you people do is force us to be as violent and stupid as you are in order to fight you. I'd prefer not to turn into my enemies, if it's all the same to you. Go on, do what good you can. I think you'll be disappointed.

MARIAN. We'll see about that. *(She starts out, hesitates.)*

ROBIN. What's the matter? Do you want an escort?
LITTLE JOHN.

MARIAN. I'm perfectly safe on my father's land—it's
Little John who'd be in danger.

ROBIN. Suit yourself. *(MARIAN starts to go again,
stops.)*

MARIAN. I want you to know that it's all right about the
gowns. Cutting them up. And thank you. For letting me
go. And for being relatively decent to me. It's idiotic, I
know, to be thanking you for such a thing, but I am.

ROBIN. You're right. It IS idiotic.

*(She looks at him, seems about to say something, changes her mind,
turns and goes out. LITTLE JOHN appears with WILL
SCARLET and DAVEY.)*

LITTLE JOHN. You want us, Robin?

ROBIN. You and Davey follow her and make sure she
gets home. And mind she doesn't see you.

LITTLE JOHN. I'll make myself small. C'mon, Davey.

DAVEY. Yo. *(They follow her out.)*

WILL SCARLET. Let her go, did you?

ROBIN. Of course I let her go. What did you expect me
to do?

·WILL SCARLET. Oh, you did right. We got no business
with the rich but to get back what they steal. Don't you be
feelin' sorry for one of them, now. They got the luxury to
do that for themselves.

ROBIN. Did you hear that?

WILL SCARLET. What? That Quigley woman laughing?
I've taken to stuffing socks in my ears. Come on, Robin,

there's plenty of pretty women in the world. You got to be cheerful for the poor folk.

ROBIN. I'm fine. I just felt a chill.

WILL SCARLET. Don't catch cold. You'll catch your death and then what'll we do? You watch.

ROBIN. I'll watch. *(WILL SCARLET goes. ROBIN thinks.)*

ALAN. *(To one side, sings.)*
I CANNOT SEE HER WESTWARD
I CANNOT SEE HER SOUTH
I CANNOT TOUCH MY TRUE LOVE NOW
I CANNOT KISS HER MOUTH
AND LONELY IS THE GRASSY GLEN
AND LONELY IS THE SEA
AND LONELY IS THE WILDWOOD DEEP
WHEN SHE IS GONE FROM ME
WHEN SHE IS GONE FROM ME.

(ROBIN goes out as the song is ending, and as the lights dim, the DARK MONK appears, watching him. Sound of the pipes. Darkness.)

END OF ACT ONE

ACT TWO
Scene 8

A crowd gathers. Music. Nottingham Fair. PURVIS THE PED-
DLER on a rostrum speaks to the crowd.

PURVIS THE PEDDLER. Hiya hiya hiya. Purvis the Peddler here with a wondrous thing to tell you of, a remedy
for all ills, a miracle of rare device. Do you suffer, my
friend, from all the evil in God's world? Do you see every
day what horrors have been perpetrated upon hapless,
suffering humanity? Look here, right here at Nottingham Fair, look at the evidence—

(The Three Unfortunate Men have appeared: BLIND BENNY,
DEAF DANNY, and DUMB DUGGAN.)

BLIND BENNY. I am blind.

DEAF DANNY. I am deaf.

DUMB DUGGAN. *(Holding up a sign which says I AM*
DUMM.) UHHHHHH UHHHHHHHHHHHHHHH
UHHHHHHHHHHHHHHHHHHHHHHHHHHHH

PURVIS THE PEDDLER. *(Going down the line to slap, poke and*
handle roughly each as he refers to them.) Do I have something
that can make Blind Benny see? Do I have something
that can make Deaf Danny hear? Do I have something
that can make Dumb Duggan sing? NO. I DO NOT.
I'VE GOT SOMETHING MUCH BETTER THAN

THAT. I'VE GOT THE CURE FOR ALL OF YOUR TROUBLES, ALL OF 'EM—I'VE GOT THE FAMOUS, ANCIENT SUMERIAN REMEDY—YE OLDE FUZZO. Yes, Ye Olde Fuzzo. Ye Olde Fuzzo will solve all your problems. Do your feet hurt? Does your nose run? Are your children ugly? Does your dog pee on the Vicar's leg? Just rub on a little of YE OLDE FUZZO and you'll never care again. Forget your troubles and get OLDE FUZZO, you're gonna chase all your cares away. One shot of YE OLDE FUZZO and you'll be peein' on the Vicar yourself! THIS lady looks like she could use a little OLDE FUZZO. Want to forget your husband, madame? I would, if I was you. Or you, sir, want to eliminate that bald spot that's spread all over your head? Rub a little of YE OLDE FUZZO on it and you'll feel like Leo the Lion. You, Miss, plagued with that troublesome thing, virginity? Come backstage with me for a little treatment of YE OLDE FUZZO, and we'll get rid of that for good. YE OLDE FUZZO, the wonder remedy of the ancients! And now, here for your delight and edification while I and my unfortunate friends sell OLDE FUZZO in the audience, are the lovely and more lovely THREE MAIDS OF TUX-FORD! Let's hear it for them!

(Applause and cheers. Out come THE THREE MAIDS to sing and dance while PURVIS and his three unfortunate men sell YE OLDE FUZZO in the crowd.)

THE THREE MAIDS. *(singing)*
OOHHHHHHHHHHHHHHHHHHHHHHHHHHHH
WE ARE THREE MAIDS OF TUXFORD

WE SING A TUXFORD SONG
THAT LIFE IS VERY SHORT MY LOVE
AND DEATH IS VERY LONG
WE LOVE TO ROMP AMONG THE TREES
AND PLAY WITH ALL THE BIRDS
WE'D LIKE TO SAY OUR PRAYERS FOR YOU
BUT WE FORGOT THE WORDS
OHHHHHHHHHHHHHHHH
GOD HELP THE POOR AND SICK
GOD BLESS THE WEAK AND YEARNING
AND GOD HELP THE FILTHY RICH
WHEN THEY IN HELL ARE BURNING.
(Repeat the chorus. Applause. The MAIDS go off, throwing kisses.)

PURVIS THE PEDDLER. *(back on the rostrum)* Thank you girls, thank you, aren't they lovely, yes, fans, you saw it here first, the Three Maids of Tuxford. They'll be back in just a minute, they've just gone off to rub YE OLDE FUZZO all over their soft young voluptuous girlish tender bodies, sorry you can't see it, it's quite a sight. YE OLDE FUZZO, my friends, does for you what life does, only much quicker, and you're so totally bezunkered that you don't notice it happening, and thus, unlike life, it's absolutely painless. Now I want to counsel all you poor and wretched people out there, who think your lot is so bad: Folks, folks, poverty is an illusion, sickness and pain are but fantasies of the spirit, rub on a little forgetfullness with YE OLDE FUZZO and you'll never care again. And to prove it to you now, here, once again, after a thorough application of YE OLDE FUZZO, the curse of virginity removed from them forever, are the THREE

MAIDS OF TUXFORD, LET'S HEAR IT FOR THEM, YAHHHHHHHH!

THREE OLD MAIDS OF TUXFORD. *(Dancing out in identical costumes to the young maids, but now grotesquely old.)*
OHHHHHHHHHHHHHHHHHHHHHHHHHHHHH
WE ARE THREE MAIDS OF TUXFORD
WE SING A TUXFORD SONG
THAT LIFE IS VERY SHORT MY LOVE
AND DEATH IS VERY LONG—
WHENEVER WE FEEL BLUE AND GRAY
AND LICE CREEP THROUGH OUR HAIR
WE RUB ON YE OLDE FUZZO AND
BEFORE LONG WE DON'T CARE.
OHHHHHHHHHHHHHHHHHH
GOD HELP THE OLD AND FRAIL
THE HUNGRY AND FORGOTTEN
FOR HE'LL BE TORTURING THE RICH
WHEN YOU AND I ARE ROTTEN.
(Repeat the chorus. They stagger off.)

PURVIS THE PEDDLER. Thank you ladies, aren't they interesting. Yes. Now, who more among ye will buy a bottle of YE OLDE FUZZO, the WONDER STUFFE? You, Sam the Rag?

SAM THE RAG. Got no money.

PURVIS THE PEDDLER. That's all right, just give me your teeth, we make dice out of 'em, sell 'em for curiosities. You, Mitch the Miller?

MITCH THE MILLER. Will it cure the upper thigh rot?

PURVIS THE PEDDLER. No, but it'll make you forget your private parts entirely. You, Bell the Tinker?

BELL THE TINKER. I think it's a racket.

PURVIS THE PEDDLER. Of course it's a racket. This is business, my friend, that's how we do things. What'd you expect? A big kiss? You, Eadom, will you take some?

EADOM. Will it bring my dead wife back to life?

PURVIS THE PEDDLER. Positively not. Have no worry on that score, she will remain entirely dead, I guarantee it, or your money back. You, Arthur O'Bland, will you buy some?

ARTHUR O'BLAND. Will it make my face interestin' to the women?

PURVIS THE PEDDLER. Are you kidding? It'll eat your face off entirely. They won't be able to take their eyes off you. What about you, Cootie the Drunk?

COOTIE THE DRUNK. I think yer fulla pig flop.

PURVIS THE PEDDLER. Ah, you've found my secret out, Cootie, but then, ain't we all? Dust we are, and dust we do return to, and you know what the dust is made of, don't you? It's nine-tenths pig flop. And what about you, Flint the Beggar?

FLINT. Will it give me back my legs?

PURVIS THE PEDDLER. No, but if you rub some on your arms, it'll make them fall off, too, and then you'll be symmetrical again.

GWENNY. I think you're a disgusting, horrible, evil man, Purvis the Peddler. Why are you doing this? And where did you come from, anyway? You ain't from around here, I hope.

PURVIS THE PEDDLER. The pretty little girl asks a very good question, and it deserves an answer, and you know, Gwenny Gwillum, my sweet, I was about to ask you the

very same thing, for do you know where you did come
from, and why you're doing what you do? You don't, and
you can't, and you'll keep on doing it anyway, and not
know why, and when your suffering is over you will lay
down and die, a little scared and a lot relieved, and more
will be born squallin' the same day to fall in the traps you
fell in, and they won't know where they come from or
what they're doin any more than you did, and they'll die,
too, and all go the same place, so my message to you, my
dear sweet friends, is to rub on YE OLDE FUZZO of
forgetfulness, and let the world pass you by, my love, let
it pass you right by, and let them that want to think they
rule ye go on and think they rule ye, for the truth is that ye
and they and all that was and is and will be is ruled by the
one great king with the head like a skull, who eats the
children of the earth like they was onions, and belches up
their grief like gas and eats some more, world without
end, AMEN.

MITCH THE MILLER. BOOOOOOOOOOOOOOO.

CROWD. BOOOO. BOOOOOOOOOOO. *(They throw
cabbages and tomatoes at him and run him off the stage until it is
deserted, and only FLINT THE BEGGAR remains. He picks up
the cabbages and tomatoes and wheels himself out, and as he does
so, ALAN sings:)*

ALAN.
HELP ME DRINK MY WINE, SHE SAID,
LET ME SING MY SONG.
LIFE IS VERY SHORT, SHE SAID,
DEATH IS VERY LONG.

Scene 9

A room at SIR STEPHEN'S. He is playing jacks. MARIAN appears, still in rags.

MARIAN. Father?

SIR STEPHEN. *(greatly startled)* What? Who? What the devil are you doing here? GUARD!

MARIAN. Daddy, it's ME. Marian. Your daughter, MARIAN.

SIR STEPHEN. Marian?

MARIAN. Yes.

SIR STEPHEN. Are you sure?

MARIAN. Of course I'm sure. Don't you recognize me?

SIR STEPHEN. What have they done to you?

MARIAN. Nothing. I'm quite well, really.

SIR STEPHEN. But what's that thing you're wearing? It looks like something the dog spewed.

MARIAN. They took my clothes, is all.

SIR STEPHEN. Oh, the SWINE, the dirty SWINE, they've ravished you.

MARIAN. No they haven't.

SIR STEPHEN. Don't lie to me, dear.

MARIAN. They haven't, I swear.

SIR STEPHEN. Well, why not? What are they, a bunch of maydoodles?

MARIAN. *(hugging him)* Oh, Daddy, I'm so glad to see you.

SIR STEPHEN. There, there, my little doodie. My little baby cakelet. Daddy's little lump of dung. Oh, my sweetie, oh, my sweetiekins, let me look at you, let me touch you, let me kiss you. Gadzook, it smells like a small horse died in your dress.

MARIAN. Daddy, listen, I've discovered a terrible thing.

SIR STEPHEN. Ygad, have they got you pregnant?

MARIAN. NO, Daddy, now listen. Did you know there are peasants on our estates so poor they eat rats?

SIR STEPHEN. Well, you know, rats aren't so bad, if you fricassee them in olive oil, they're rather tasty, I hear.

MARIAN. No, Daddy, some of these people have no homes, they've nothing to eat, they're sick, some are dying—

SIR STEPHEN. Who's been telling you this rubbish?

MARIAN. It's not rubbish, Daddy, I've seen them.

SIR STEPHEN. Actors. Paid actors. Say anything for money. You've been taken in, dear. No one's starving around here.

MARIAN. Daddy, I've just SEEN them--one of them is Flint, do you remember Flint, that used to tell me stories in the barn?

SIR STEPHEN. That degenerate that used to bounce you on his lap? Hah. I got rid of that one, had him drafted, he's long gone.

MARIAN. But Daddy—

SIR STEPHEN. Oh, Marian, Marian, tax not your brain over that which cannot concern an innocent young thingie like yourself, pregnant though you may be. Now you just take off that foul-smelling thing there and have the servants burn it.

MARIAN. But you've got to do something about this, Daddy.

SIR STEPHEN. It's just a temporary economic phenomenon, dear, they'll be all right in the long run. The wealth of the privileged classes will eventually drool down onto the poor.

MARIAN. Drool down?

SIR STEPHEN. Prince John says that in a healthy economy the wealth of the superior people will drool down through the nation's cracks and eventually dribble onto the lower orders.

MARIAN. Just how long is this drooling supposed to take?

SIR STEPHEN. Not long. A few hundred years at most.

MARIAN. But they're hungry NOW, Daddy.

SIR STEPHEN. Have those ruffians been taking advantage of your tender little heart? If God wanted these people to have what we have, God would take it from us and give it to them. They've managed to survive this long. The poor are always with us, scripture says.

MARIAN. It also says it's harder for a rich man to enter heaven than for a camel to pass through the eye of a needle.

SIR STEPHEN. That is merely a metaphor. You've been brain-scrubbed, dear, it happens to kidnap and ravish victims all the time, it will pass, believe me. Among wealth, it's easy to forget.

MARIAN. I DON'T WANT TO FORGET.

SIR STEPHEN. Why don't you have a bath and we can

share some lime sherbet I saved from dinner. I was going to give it to the dog, but now that you're here—

MARIAN. You're not going to do anything, are you? Those people live in absolute squalor right under your nose while you're sharing lime sherbet with the dog, you'd better do SOMETHING about it before they march in here and cut all our throats, I can't imagine why they haven't done it a long time ago, but then, I'm one of YOU, aren't I? I think like you do. That's how YOU'D solve a problem.

SIR STEPHEN. You're raving, dear, you're quite hysterical. Your Aunt Penelope was carried off on three or four occasions by various gardeners and house guests and such, and it did the same thing to HER brain, what there was of it—all she could talk about afterwards was wart hogs and yodeling.

MARIAN. If you don't do something about this, I'm going to see Prince John. He isn't a bad person, he just doesn't understand—

SIR STEPHEN. He understands much more than you do, but if you want to try, go ahead, I won't stop you, just don't go dressed like that or he'll never marry you, he'll probably have you fumigated. *(But MARIAN is already gone.)* Just like her mother. Head like a sponge. Well, Prince John'll take care of her, just needs a good tumble in the greensward. Now where did my little ball go? I was up to ninesies, I think. Here, ball. *(He wanders off.)*

ALAN. *(singing)*
I AM THE QUEEN OF POVERTY
I AM PRINCESS OF NEED
I SING MY SONG AND NO ONE HEARS

THE WORLD IS MADE OF GREED
THE WORLD IS MADE OF GREED.

Scene 10

*NottinghamCastle. BRONWEN doing exercises with GROK. A
strange woman with wild hair follows PRINCE JOHN
around as he paces.*

BRONWEN. Stop goin' back and forth, you're makin'
me dizzy.

PRINCE JOHN. I hate waiting. A sovereign should never
be kept waiting. It is necessary for a sovereign to receive
immediate gratification in all circumstances, that is
God's law. WHY haven't they found her yet?

(He turns and runs into the strange woman.)

PRINCE JOHN. And who IS this very strange person?

BRONWEN. It's the translator for Grok.

PRINCE JOHN. Who?

BRONWEN. The jester. Grok. Him.

GROK. Rigoofky? Beyucka?

PRINCE JOHN. Really? Then why hasn't she said
something?

BRONWEN. They told her not to speak unless she was
spoken to.

PRINCE JOHN. Ah. So, you're the translator, are you?

BREKKA. Shlondy?

PRINCE JOHN. Translator. Trans-la-tor. You DO speak
English?

BREKKA. Enk-leash? Oh, ENKLEZ, jes, jes, yecky
much.

GROK. Scholby knetchet der-drenchensky das Enklex?
(He punctuates this sentence with a loud raspberry sound.)

BREKKA. *(laughing immorderately)* Ya, ya, ya.

PRINCE JOHN. *(chortling in anticipation)* Was that a jest?
What did he say?

BREKKA. He say, Scholby, knetchet der-drenchensky
das Enklex? *(She punctuates with the raspberry sound.)*

PRINCE JOHN. Yes, I heard what he said, what does
it mean?

BREKKA. Oh, he say schloby—that is, Goats, or is it
Groats? —uh, knetchet—that is, eat, or maybe, feet—
Goats feets or goats eat—

GROK. *(Smiling and nodding and kissing PRINCE JOHN'S
hand.)* Shloggly yug suggoth, yeckly yukkoskly.

PRINCE JOHN. What did he say?

BREKKA. He say he is proud, sir, that in the brief time
which he has worked here for you, that you have been, to
him, sir, a constant source of excrement.

PRINCE JOHN. A what?

(The SHERIFF is trying to keep MARIAN out.)

SHERIFF. You can't go in like that, you've got to be
announced, you've got to be summoned, you've got to
be bathed—

MARIAN. Let me by, you moron.

PRINCE JOHN. Who's that? What is it? Who are you?

MARIAN. Maid Marian, of course.

PRINCE JOHN. Maid Marian? You're Maid Marian? Are you sure?

MARIAN. It really is me. I hadn't time to change.

SHERIFF. I believe it is, sire.

PRINCE JOHN. Well, she's not much good to me that way, is she? She smells like the place the elephants go to break wind.

MARIAN. Your majesty, I have very important news.

PRINCE JOHN. Oh, good. What's that?

MARIAN. There are many people in your kingdom starving to death.

PRINCE JOHN. And?

MARIAN. And they live in absolute poverty and filth.

PRINCE JOHN. And? And?

MARIAN. And, uh, we've got to do something about it.

PRINCE JOHN. We?

MARIAN. I mean, you.

PRINCE JOHN. You've been here a minute and a half, and already you're telling me how to run my kingdom. Most women take a day or two at least.

MARIAN. If you could just see them, sire.

PRINCE JOHN. I don't care to see them. It's all part of God's plan.

MARIAN. I don't belive it's God's plan for people to live like animals.

PRINCE JOHN. But most of them ARE animals. There's nothing I can do about it. Am I my brother's keeper?

MARIAN. But you're in charge, aren't you, until King Richard—

PRINCE JOHN. BITE your tongue.

MARIAN. If you don't swear to do something about this, I warn you, I'll never consent to marry you. I'll die first.

BRONWEN. You certainly will.

PRINCE JOHN. Bronwen.

BRONWEN. Sorry. Lost my head.

PRINCE JOHN. Look, I'm not an unreasonble man. Why don't you tell me just what specific actions you'd have me take?

MARIAN. Uh, well, reduce the taxes on the poor by half. Double taxes for the rich. Provide food and clothing for those unable to provide it for themselves—use the tax money from the rich to finance this—it won't cost you a cent—you can distribute things through the local churches, I'm sure they'd help—and it will provide jobs for those able to work—helping those that can't.

PRINCE JOHN. All right. Fine.

MARIAN. Fine? You mean, you'll do it?

PRINCE JOHN. We'll write it up and issue it a proclamation—you can oversee the program yourself, and put in anything else you think is necessary, within reason.

MARIAN. That's wonderful. I just KNEW that deep down you were a compassionate man, I KNEW it—and it will work, you'll see, and the people will love you for it, and—

PRINCE JOHN. Wait a minute, I'm not finished, there's a condition.

MARIAN. What condition?

PRINCE JOHN. I'll initiate these reforms IF the outlaw Robin Hood will first turn himself in to the Sheriff.

MARIAN. I don't see the connection. Don't you want to

do good for your people?

PRINCE JOHN. Of course I do. I want to do so much good there'll be no more need for Robin Hood to do it FOR me. If he really loves the people, he'll give himself up for them, won't he?

MARIAN. What would happen to him if he did?

PRINCE JOHN. What difference does it make? He's a thief, we can't just let him go. Or do you care more about keeping this malefactor safe than you do about your precious poor?

(SALLY has come in with her enormous tea tray and stands waiting to be noticed, afraid to interrupt. PRINCE JOHN is pacing but she avoids him.)

MARIAN. Of course not. But, still—

PRINCE JOHN. And on the day he turns himself in, you and I can become, well, very close?

MARIAN. I will agree to marry you then, if you wish.

PRINCE JOHN. Yes, we'll negotiate that. Sheriff, have the proclamation drawn up posthaste. Put in whatever she likes.

SHERIFF. Do you think that's wise, sire? I mean—

(The CONSTABLE bursts in, knocking SALLY and the tea tray in every direction.)

CONSTABLE. HARK! ABAST! AN URGENT EJACULATION FROM A BROAD! AN AUSPICIOUS EPUSTLE FROM ASTRIA.

PRINCE JOHN. What are you blathering about? Give me

that. *(He snatches the message and rips it open.)* Dear Prince,
We regret to inform you of the demise of your brother,
King Richard the Lion Hearted, in a rat-infested
dungeon in Austria, on Thursday last. The King is Dead.
Long Live the King. Your friend, Crown Prince Farfal.
Good Christ, he's finally DEAD. RICHARD IS DEAD.
MY LOATHESOME PSYCHOTIC BROTHER IS
FINALLY PUSHING UP WORMS. I'M KING, I'M
KING, OH, ISN'T THIS A HAPPY DAY? *(He looks around.
Everyone else looks perfectly miserable.)* What's the matter?
The King is DEAD. Why don't you look happy? Come
on, I want to see some HAPPY around here. This looks
like an autopsy. I want some jubilation. That's an
order.

BRONWEN. *(dry)* Hip hip. *(pause)*

OTHERS. *(weakly)* Hooray.

PRINCE JOHN. That's better. What is this mess here?
Sally, clean that up. I'm going and get fitted for the
crown. Oh, what JOY. And don't forget the proclamation! La la la la. *(He skips out. All are grim.)*

GROK. *(Pointing out after the PRINCE.)* Schlubsky nudnik
supremsky monarchik?

BREKKA. Ya. Nudnick giguntsky cheesisky nuvem,
der yutz.

GROK. In that case, it seems to me that, on the whole,
it's time for us to pack up our tents and debouch, as
it were.

BREKKA. I agree. *(They go out. BRONWEN looks at
MARIAN.)*

BRONWEN. If you listen close you can hear the
kingdom decomposing. *(She begins helping SALLY clean up*

the mess. MARIAN stands there.)

Scene 11

*Nottingham Square. REDCAP and CRUIKSHANK appear with
long trumpeter horns, which neither handles or plays very
well. The CONSTABLE appears between them.*

Constable. ATTENTION. ATTENTION. HARK.

*(The soldiers blow tremendous trumpet blasts. The CONSTABLE
jumps and nearly dies, recovers.)*

Constable. HEAR YE, HEAR YE, AND KNOW
THEE WELL BY ALL THESE PRESENTS, THAT TO
WHOM IT MAY CONCERN, AND WHATSOEVER
MAY BEFALL THE NONCE, HARK, A PROCLA-
MATION—

*(The trumpet blasts again. The proclamation unrolls from the
CONSTABLE'S hands, heavily weighted, and falls with a thud on
his feet.)*

Constable. OWWWWWWWWW. ZOOKERS. Oh. A
PROCLAMATION BY HIS MAJESTY THE GREAT
AND BENEVOLENT PRINCE JOHN.

(The trumpets again, one in each of the CONSTABLE'S ears.)

CONSTABLE. HEAR YE ALL THIS PROCLAMA-TION! *(He covers his ears. The trumpets don't sound.)*

CRUIKSHANK. Well, read it.

CONSTABLE. *(temporarily deafened)* What?

CRUIKSHANK. Read the proclamation.

CONSTABLE. I can't read.

CRUIKSHANK. Then say SOMETHING, don't leave us standin' here with these bloody damn trumpets and nothin' to proclaim.

CONSTABLE. A PROCLAMATION CONCERNING ROBIN HOOD. PROCLAIMING THAT IF THE AFORESHKINNED ROBIN HOOD—

CRUIKSHANK. Aforesaid.

CONSTABLE. If the aforesaid Robin Hood doth present himself and give himself up to Prince John and the Sheriff and all the authorities on market day next in the courtyard of Nottingham castle, then Prince John in good faith will desist in all plans to cut down ye Sherwood Forest, and will furthermore institute programs to educate and feed the poor, provide doctors and shelter for all who need same, halve the tax on the poor and double it on the rich, end conscription of persons into the army, and perform certain assorted other semi-humanitarian acts which I forget, all this contingent upon the surrendering of said Robin Hood on market day next. *(He's gone dry.)*

REDCAP. King Richard.

CONSTABLE. What?

REDCAP. King Richard.

CONSTABLE. Oh. Prince John doth further proclaim that he has news of good King Richard the Lion Hearted,

which he will share with the general populace at that
same time and place, hear ye, hear ye, sis boom bah,
world without end, amen.

(The trumpet blasts. The CONSTABLE falls over.)

ALAN. *(singing)*
AS I WAS WALKIN' SO LONELY
I SAW THREE RAVENS IN A TREE
THEY WAS AS BLACK AS BLACK COULD BE
WITH A DOWNE DERRY DERRY DOWNE...

Scene 12

The forest. ROBIN sits alone among the leaves. Forest sounds. As
he begins to speak. MARIAN appears behind and listens.
He seems not to notice.

ROBIN.
These woods will die, ways will be found to kill them.
They think the forest's endless but it has
an end, and when the beauty's gone, it's gone
forever. Who destroys the living green
destroyeth me and all my kind. In greenwood
does the secret live, among the twisted
vines and branches lurks the wood-god in
the leaves who dies and is reborn and dies
again. It's mortal sin to kill the woods.

We come from woods, they are the tangled remnants
of the garden God once planted. When we lay
them waste we ravage God, ourselves and our
connectedness to time. They die, the people
die, and violence eats up my soul
and makes me one with them I ought to hate.
I am the body of disorder and the chaos,
and the beast inside my head, the animal
which must get out somehow—
*(By the last line he is aware that something is watching him, and
then, very quick, like an animal, he hurls himself in MARIAN'S
direction and throttles her.)*

MARIAN. AAAAAAHHHHHHHHHHHHHH.

ROBIN. Good God, I might have broken your neck.
What are you doing here? It's dangerous to eavesdrop on
a wanted man.

MARIAN. *(pulling away, shaken)* Yes, I can see that. Well,
aren't you even going to apologize?

ROBIN. For your stupidity? How did you get here?

MARIAN. I saw Quigley at Nottingham market and she
brought me.

ROBIN. I don't know why she doesn't advertise my
whereabouts upon her undergarments—they'd get max-
imum exposure there.

MARIAN. She was just trying to help.

ROBIN. What do you want?

MARIAN. To make sure you knew about the proclamation.

ROBIN. The whole kingdom knows of it.

MARIAN. Will you turn yourself in?

ROBIN. Would that please you?

MARIAN. Does my opinion matter?

ROBIN. I don't know. You seem to have come a long distance to give it. Was it your idea, this proclamation business?

MARIAN. I made a bargain with Prince John.

ROBIN. It's good of you to bargain with my life.

MARIAN. It didn't properly concern your life, it concerned certain reforms. And MY life.

ROBIN. Well, we know what I'm supposed to give up, for these alleged reforms. What do YOU give up?

MARIAN. I agree to marry him.

ROBIN. Oh, a trifle, just your body.

MARIAN. It's MY body, to give as I choose. He can't own my soul.

ROBIN. He's always owned your soul. And I wouldn't hold your breath, waiting for him to marry you.

MARIAN. If he doesn't, so much the better.

ROBIN. If you don't want to marry him then why do you—

MARIAN. FOR THOSE PEOPLE YOU SHOWED ME.

ROBIN. You'd agreed to marry him before that.

MARIAN. I didn't have much choice, did I? Anyway, that's how it looked to me then. No one asked me what I wanted. At least now it might serve some purpose. It's no more sacrifice than you'll make.

ROBIN. What makes you think I'm going?

MARIAN. Don't you trust him to keep his word?

ROBIN. I trust him not to. Still. Shame to waste such a lovely body as yours on that moron. Your soul also has something to be said for it. Needs a bit more work, but then, so does mine.

MARIAN. You've made me a different person, you know.

ROBIN. No, that's too easy. You must do that for yourself. *(They are quite close. He looks at her, and it appears that something is going to happen—then ROBIN'S head jerks up.)* Will Stutely, what are you doing behind that tree?

(WILL STUTLEY is sticking his head out, embarrssed.)

WILL STUTELY. I was just, uh, um, I was--

ROBIN. Yes, all right, I want you to take Marian safely back to Nottingham and then clear out of there, you understand? Take her the short way, I'm going down the old path in the dark part of the wood, I want to think some on the way. Go on.

WILL STUTELY. You're going, then?

(One by one the MERRY MEN begin to appear from behind trees, in much concern.)

ROBIN. You have some objection to that?

LITTLE JOHN. We've decided, Robin, we cannot let you.

ROBIN. Oh, you've decided, have you? And which of you is going to stop me?

MARIAN. I've changed my mind. They're right. You mustn't go.

ROBIN. Will Stutely, get this woman to Nottingham, or to her father's house, or anyplace she cares to go, but get her out of here. You're in charge while I'm gone. Take care of these poor ninnies for me. They're a sorry lot, but I've developed some affection for them. *(They are all looking at him.)* Well, don't stand there looking foolish at me. Go on about your business. I've better things to do than watch you gape.

(One by one they turn and go. WILL STUTELY takes MARIAN. ROBIN alone. He picks up a handful of leaves. Wood sounds, faint. Then, very quietly, the eerie sound of the pipes, ROBIN looks up. The DARK MONK is there, watching him.)

DARK MONK. Robin Hood.

ROBIN. I haven't time, I'm sorry, I must go to Nottingham today. If you're in need, my men will help you.

DARK MONK. It's you I need. I hear you make great trouble for Prince John.

ROBIN. I mean no harm to him or anyone. I only mean to help them he takes advantage of.

DARK MONK. I think you also mean to help yourself.

ROBIN. I help myself and others when I do what's right.

DARK MONK. And how can you be sure you don't do greater harm than good, defying England's rightful king?

ROBIN. Prince John is not the king. Richard the Lion Heart is king.

DARK MONK. But there is another, more powerful than he, who they say has conquered even great King Richard.

ROBIN. And who might that be?

DARK MONK. They say that Death has conquered him.

ROBIN. I don't wish to be rude to you, but I have important business this day at—

DARK MONK. *(Putting his stick in ROBIN'S way, a sudden and rather violent gesture.)* You have no business more important than your business with me.

ROBIN. Let me pass.

DARK MONK. When my business is done.

ROBIN. Are you some agent of the Sheriff, come to keep me from appearing so the people will think I've betrayed them?

DARK MONK. No, the Sheriff works for me. Many do work for me that do not know it.

ROBIN. You must let me pass. I will fight you if I must.

DARK MONK. You'll lose. All who fight me lose. I win all battles.

ROBIN. I think your wits are turned.

DARK MONK. Do you care to try me?

(ROBIN tries to move around him, but the MONK moves with him. Sound of the pipes. The MONK whacks him hard with his stick.)

ROBIN. OWWWWWWWW.

DARK MONK. Oh, did I hurt you? I'm so sorry.

ROBIN. I have no wish to harm you, but I will let no man stop me this day.

DARK MONK. But I am more than man, and less. I am

all and nothing too. I rule this world, and I have come to claim you. *(ROBIN tries to pass again, but the MONK whacks him harder with the stick.)*

ROBIN. You will anger me.

DARK MONK. But anger is a sin. Surely the saintly Robin Hood would not commit a sin, except perhaps for robbery and murder. *(ROBIN makes a quick move, but the MONK is extremely skilled and agile, and whacks him several times, playing.)* The great Robin Hood is angry. He is also very slow and rather stupid, I see.

ROBIN. Listen to me, I'm on my way to turn myself in. If you wish to do me harm, then simply let me pass— Prince John will do more harm to me than you can.

DARK MONK. I will let you pass, on one condition.

ROBIN. And what is that?

DARK MONK. That I might come along with you. Make an alliance with me, Robin, you cannot win against the dead.

ROBIN. You're quite mad, but you're very good with that stick, and I don't care to kill you. You may come along with me if you like.

DARK MONK. *(Gesturing ironically for ROBIN to go ahead.)* That's very kind of you. Shall we go? *(They go out together, ROBIN uneasy.)*

ALAN. *(Singing softly.)*
WHERE SHALL WE DINE TODAY SAYS ONE
DOWN WHERE THE WILLOW BROOK DOES RUN
THERE LIES A DEAD MAN IN THE SUN
WITH A DOWNE DERRY DERRY DOWNE.

Scene 13

Courtyard of Nottingham Castle. A crowd gathers, among them, FLINT, ELLEN, JENNY, GWENNY, OLD GUMMY GRANNY, and a good many old women and cloaked persons. The CONSTABLE with REDCAP and CRUIKSHANK. The SHERIFF scans the crowd. MARIAN and QUIGELY.

SHERIFF. Sound the trumpets again.
JENNY. Do you think he's coming, Ellen?
ELLEN. I hope he doesn't.
JENNY. Maybe the dead thing got him in the woods.
ELLEN. Don't say that.
SHERIFF. His royal majesty, Prince John.
CONSTABLE. PRINCE JOHN.

(The soldiers blow their trumpets, nearly deafening PRINCE JOHN. BRONWEN wheels the old QUEEN in.)

GWENNY. Look, Granny, there's Prince John.
OLD GUMMY GRANNY. The one that looks like a snake? Yuk. Ugly, ugly.
GWENNY. Shush, Granny, you'll get us killt.
PRINCE JOHN. Well, where is he? Where is this hero Robin Hood? Do you see, my poor foolish people how he mocks you? He dare not show his face to us. So much for your saviour. So much for your great Robin Hood.

89

We can wait no longer. We must do our royal business. Where is this saintly coward?

(ROBIN appears with the DARK MONK.)

ROBIN. He's here. *(Much exclamation from the crowd.)*

PRINCE JOHN. And have you come unarmed, as we did stipulate?

ROBIN. And alone, except for this old Monk.

PRINCE JOHN. Good. Seize him. *(ROBIN allows RED-CAP and CRUIKSHANK to seize him, which is awkward, as they still have their horns.)*

REDCAP. Sorry, sir.

PRINCE JOHN. Don't apologize to him, you idiot. Now we're going to get some things settled around here. For one thing, we're going to double taxes on the poor, and eliminate them altogether for the nobility. It's about time you people stopped spunging off the upper classes and started paying your way around here. For another thing, all vagrants will be executed. Any person speaking ill of the royal family will be hung by his ears. And Sherwood Forest will be cut down and made into a tennis club.

MARIAN. But you promised—

PRINCE JOHN. Oh, do shut up. Did you think I was going to let you and this hooligan run my kingdom for me? And as for Robin Hood, he shall be tortured, castrated, hung, shot full of arrows, torn apart by horses, and then killed until he is dead.

ROBIN. By what authority do you do this?

PRINCE JOHN. Executive privilege. I have just received word that my brother, King Richard the Lion Hearted, has died in Austria. *(The crowd is shocked and horrified.)* I have shed a number of tears over this in private. But, life must go on. And since my brother has left no issue, being, as I always suspected, something of a maydoodle, I am, thus, ergo and forsooth, declared the new King of England. You may cheer now if you wish. *(Nothing. Silence.)*

DARK MONK. One moment, please.

PRINCE JOHN. One moment? Who dares to say One moment? Who dares to interrupt the monarch?

DARK MONK. The true monarch.

PRINCE JOHN. I am the true monarch.

DARK MONK. My kingdom is greater than yours.

PRINCE JOHN. Treason. Seize this thing. Seize him.

(The SHERIFF and the CONSTABLE move towards the DARK MONK, who pulls down his hood, revealing a hideous skeleton face, hissing at them, stopping them in their tracks.)

DARK MONK. Do you dare lay hands upon Death himself? *(The people scream and back away. Even the SHERIFF is spooked.)*

PRINCE JOHN. Good Lord, what are you people afraid of? This is not Death. This is a man in a skeleton mask. Did you never trick or treat? Have you not been to the theatre? Can't you see this creature is not dead?

DARK MONK. You contradict yourself—you just told these people I was dead.

PRINCE JOHN. I said my brother, King Richard, was dead.

DARK MONK. Then you told a lie, Johnny, shame on you.

(He whips off the skeleton mask to reveal KING RICHARD.)

THE PEOPLE. *(Exclaiming, kneeling, jumping up and down.)*
KING RICHARD. IT'S KING RICHARD. WE'RE
SAVED. WE'RE SAVED.

PRINCE JOHN. I believe I'm late for my zither lessons.
(He tries to slip away.)

KING RICHARD. SEIZE HIM. *(PRINCE JOHN is seized by
REDCAP and CRUIKSHANK.)*

PRINCE JOHN. Get your hands off me, I'm wealthy. Stop
that.

MARIAN. Oh, King Richard, your majesty, we're all so
happy to see you. We've waited such a long time for you.
Now your people will be freed from their burdens. Now
the tax won't be doubled on the poor, and the trees won't
be cut down. Now the people will have food to eat.

THE PEOPLE. YAAAYYYYYYYYYYYYYYYYY.

KING RICHARD. *(Leaping up onto the rostrum.)* My loyal
subjects. I have returned from my long captivity in Austria to save my people and my kingdom from this wicked
brother of mine, who has been paying off my captors for
years and plotting my death. Unbeknownst to you, I have
been in your midst for some time, living among you as a
peddler in your cities, and a poor monk in the forest, and
I have come to know you well. I wished to see what my
brother had accomplished in this kingdom in my absence.
Well, now I can see. He has done nothing. I am, as you
will learn, a very different sort of ruler. I have seen the
poverty you live in, my people, and I am appalled by it.
Do you know why you live in such degradation? It's
because the laziness and self-indulgence of my brother

has drooled down upon you. I promise you I'm going to change all this. He proposes to cut down Sherwood Forest to make a tennis thing. A TENNIS THING. I would take no such frivolous action. I will cut down the forest, but I will sell the wood to finance another glorious Crusade to the Holy Land, for the greater glory of God and England, and for the salvation of the eternal souls of its people. He proposes to double your taxes. I propose instead to triple them. It's a challenge that you need, a sense that someone you can respect is in charge. And fear not, the money will go to a good cause—the Bulgarians are massing on the banks of the Danube, and this worm, my brother, has neglected our defenses shamefully.

MARIAN. But what about the food? These people are going hungry.

KING RICHARD. I will not insult my subjects by offering them food. My people are a proud people, they do not accept handouts. And I will do more yet for my people—I will give you spectacle, and law and order. We shall take this cretin, my brother John, whom I dearly love, but for the sake of justice, truth, and liberty, we will take this beloved cretinous brother of mine and hang him on the highest tree, right beside the swinging corpse of this unspeakable vermin who calls himself Robin Hood.

MARIAN. Your majesty, you can't, you mustn't do that, the people look upon you as their saviour—

KING RICHARD. And well they should. Indeed, I am. I'm saving them from thieves and trouble-makers and
incompetence in high places, among other things. Now speak to me no more, I listen not to women, they remind

me of my mother, the dear old queen, who, I fear, alas, in my long absence, must have finally kicked her royal bucket, as the old hag must be two hundred if she's a day. I mourn for her, great lady that she was, the only living soul I ever feared in my entire life, god bless her and good riddance.

PRINCE JOHN. Actually, Dickie, I'm afraid she's right over there.

KING RICHARD. Over there?

(QUEEN ELEANOR appears from behind BRONWEN, in all the majesty of her wrath.)

QUEEN ELEANOR. Old hag, am I? Kicked the royal bucket, did I? Two hundred, am I?

KING RICHARD. Uh, now, Mother, listen—

QUEEN ELEANOR. You little beanhead. Neither one of you was ever worth the poop you shat. How a woman like me ever whelped a pair of peepshow geeks like you, I'll never understand.

KING RICHARD. Mother—

QUEEN ELEANOR. *(Grabbing RICHARD by the ear.)* Now you listen to me.

KING RICHARD. OWWWWWWWWWWWWW.

QUEEN ELEANOR. Johnny will NOT be executed, do you hear?

KING RICHARD. Yes, Mother.

PRINCE JOHN. Good show, Mum. Squeeze harder.

QUEEN ELEANOR. *(Grabbing JOHN also by the ear.)* And the forest will NOT be cut down.

PRINCE JOHN. OWWWWWWWWWWWWWWW.

QUEEN ELEANOR. I like the forest, the forest is nice, I go hunting there, and it's an excellent place to have sexual intercourse. And you, Dickie, are going to stay home for a change and spend some time with your mother instead of running about butchering Bulgarians, have you got that?

KING RICHARD. Yes, Mother.

MARIAN. What about Robin Hood? Will you pardon Robin Hood, too?

QUEEN ELEANOR. Robin Hood? Certainly not. Off with his head. Chop it right off. We do not tolerate dissent in my kingdom. This country has gone to pot. Look at all these filthy people. What a mess. Look at all these ugly old women. I've never seen so many ugly women in my life.

WILL SCARLET. *(Quite close to her, taking off his old lady wig.)* I say, have you looked in the mirror lately?

QUEEN ELEANOR. I beg your pardon?

LITTLE JOHN. *(taking off his disguise)* ALL RIGHT, MEN, IF NOBODY ELSE WILL SAVE ROBIN, IT'S UP TO US OLD WOMEN. *(Old women scattered about the crowd turn into MERRY MEN. Somebody screams. A great confused battle ensues, the crowd caught in the middle. The SHERIFF is after ROBIN, and the climax of their fight and of the battle as a whole is that he manages to impale himself on ROBIN'S blade, at the highest point on the stage, gives a genuinely horrible scream of pain, surprise and anguish and falls some distance to the ground. This moment, unlike some earlier parts of the battle, should not be funny. The rest of the action stops as all watch the SHERIFF fall. A moment. Then—)*

PRINCE JOHN. RETREAT. RETREAT. THE SHERIFF'S

DEAD. RETREAT. *(Before KING RICHARD can stop them, all the soldiers have run off, and finally RICHARD goes, too. ROBIN stares down at the dead man.)*

LITTLE JOHN. Come on, Robin, we got to run for it, the King'll get reinforcements from the castle. Robin, come on. *(ROBIN allows the MERRY MEN to get him away. MARIAN looks after them, in rather a daze. What's left of the crowd breaks up, and GWENNY, who has been sitting on a ledge, eating an apple through most of the fight, watching as if at the movies, jumps down with GRANNY.)*

GWENNY. Come on, Granny, time to clear out, show's over.

OLD GUMMY GRANNY. I was just startin' to enjoy it. Who won?

GWENNY. Lord, I don't know, but I know who lost. It's you and me that lost, love. It's always you and me. *(They go out.)*

Scene 14

The Blue Boar Inn. ALAN plays disconsolately. ELLEN and JENNY work. The MERRY MEN are scattered about, drinking, glum. COOTIE in his old spot.

ELLEN. Move yer feet, Alan, I got to mop under you.

ALAN. So there's no more sweet words between us, is there? Once it was Alan my dear and Alan my darling, and now it's Move yer feet, I got to mop. Such is love.

ELLEN. Love or no, I got to mop the floor.

FRIAR TUCK. You're too good for him, Ellen. Throw the puny thing over and come with me, I'm a sensitive man, I am, don't laugh, I've been writing a poem about meself, in fact. Would you like to hear it?

EVERYBODY. NO.

FRIAR TUCK.

I do lament that I am fat.
It is my great misfortune that
when I do bend to reach the mutton
I cannot see beyond my belly button.
When I do stretch to reach the pork
I cannot get my arms to work.
When I attempt to fill my cup
I find that I cannot get up.
It is a great mysterious sadness
that something that doth make such gladness
should be so hard to get to.

(pause)

COOTIE THE DRUNK. This poem doth suck prodigiously.

(MARIAN comes in, trailing QUIGLEY behind. All look at her.)

MARIAN. Hello.

LITTLE JOHN. Hello, miss. What be you doin' here? I hope you ain't brought no soldiers with you.

MARIAN. Of course I haven't. Gwenny said I might

find some of you here. Do you know where Robin is?

LITTLE JOHN. He's hidin', miss. They're after him everywhere.

MARIAN. They've always been after him. They're after you, and you, and all of you, but you don't seem to be hiding too seriously. Why hasn't he been doing his work? Was he wounded in the battle?

LITTLE JOHN. Oh, some, but I don't think it's that, exactly. We all did place great hopes on the return of the King, but now things is worse than ever. The Old Queen saved the forest, but she can't live much longer, and with Richard gone to fight more wars in the nether reaches of nowhere for God knows what reason, Prince John's in power again, and will be king after him, and none of the three but wouldn't rest easier with Robin's head on a platter. There be no help from high places, miss. Not for us.

MARIAN. I want to talk to Robin.

LITTLE JOHN. I've sworn to tell nobody where he is.

MARIAN. But you can tell me, I'm his friend, you know that.

LITTLE JOHN. I'd like to tell you, miss, I really would, but I can't go back on what I've sworn.

MARIAN. Will Scarlet, will you tell me?

WILL SCARLET. No.

MARIAN. Will Stutely?

WILL STUTELY. I've sworn a vow, miss. We all have.

FRIAR TUCK. I'd tell you if I knew, but I was not trusted with the secret, a fact which would offend me deeply were I not so magnanimous.

MARIAN. Is there not one man among you loves Robin

enough to break a stupid promise for his own good?

LITTLE JOHN. I expect seein' you would cheer him up a bit, he's fond of you, but I've give me word. I can't. *(pause)* Well, I be goin' off now to visit, to visit a certain person I know, and I don't want any person, now, not any person to be followin' me, because if a person was to be followin' me, secret like, without me knowin' it, with me totally unawares I was bein' followed, they might just stumble upon the whereabouts of the person I was goin' to see. Gbye Ellen. Gbye Jenny. C'mon, Will Scarlet. Now, don't anybody follow me, now, because I'm quite pre-occupied, and might fail altogether to look behind me, and Will Scarlet also, is that not right, Will?

WILL SCARLET. I might in fact be totally oblivious of anyone behind me.

LITTLE JOHN. Well, then, let's go. *(The two go out. MARIAN hesitates, then follows. The people all go to the door to look after them. FRIAR TUCK places a hand on QUIGLEY'S bottom. She slaps it away.)*

ALAN. *(singing)*
OH WHAT IS GREENER THAN THE GRASS
AND WHAT IS HIGHER THAN THE TREES
OR WHAT IS WORSE THAN WOMAN'S WISH
AND WHAT IS DEEPER THAN THE SEAS?

DEATH IS GREENER THAN THE GRASS
AND HEAVEN'S HIGHER THAN THE TREES
THE DEVIL'S WORSE THAN WOMAN'S WISH
AND HELL IS DEEPER THAN THE SEAS
AND HELL IS DEEPER THAN THE SEAS.

Scene 15

Sound of nuns singing. The PRIORY OF KIRKLEES. ROBIN sleeps on a small bed. Eerie lights and a piping sound. A GHOST appears.

GHOST. Robin Hood. It's time now, Robin, we've come to get you, my friend and I. My friend the Sheriff. Look.

(The SHERIFF appears, green and dead like the GHOST, with a bloody wound.)

GHOST. This is the second man you killed. You're bound to him for all eternity, as you are bound to me, my little boy, my little sonny. Bonny sweet Robin was all my joy. You killed me, too.

ROBIN. NOOOOOOOOOOOO.

GHOST. Kill begets kill, world without end, hate makes hate, blood makes blood, guilt makes guilt, death makes death, son kills father, father kills son, want make pain, love betrays, love kills, compassion kills, pity kills, God kills, Robin kills, Robin kills, Robin kills—

ROBIN. NOOOOOOOOOOOOO. NOOOOOOOO

(He sits up in bed, screaming. The PRIORESS appears with candle. The Spirits have vanished.)

PRIORESS. Nightmares again, my sweetie? Ohh, the bad dreams is all gone now. Here we go, some lovely supper for my boy, pea hen and Irish beans, I know it is your favorite.

ROBIN. I'm not hungry, Prioress.

PRIORESS. If you don't have a bit of something soon you'll die, my boy. Just have a taste of this. Yumm YUMMM. Twill chase them nasty nightmares right away.

ROBIN. All right. Just leave it, I'll eat it by and by.

PRIORESS. That's my little boykin. We must keep our strength up, mustn't we?

SISTER FELICITY. *(from off, indignant)* HELP. NO. YOU MUSTN'T. NO. HE ISN'T HERE.

(MARIAN appears, with an indignant and hysterical nun trying to obstruct her progress, and LITTLE JOHN and WILL SCARLET keeping her away gently.)

SISTER FELICITY. YOU MUSTN'T GO IN THERE. GOD WILL STRIKE YOU DOWN. OOOO. *(This last as LITTLE JOHN finally just picks her up carefully by the waist and holds her in the air while MARIAN passes.)*

PRIORESS. This man is not to be disturbed.

SISTER FELICITY. I tried to keep her out, but this great goon keeps touching my person.

PRIORESS. You. Put her down.

LITTLE JOHN. Yes mum. *(He does.)*

ROBIN. It's all right. Let her by.

PRIORESS. We have our rules. It's not good for your health.

ROBIN. Prioress, I will speak with the lady. You may go.

PRIORESS. If I give you a moment with this person, will you eat every bit of your supper?

ROBIN. I promise.

PRIORESS. Very well then. But watch her. I don't like the look of her at all.

ROBIN. I'll keep a careful eye on her.

PRIORESS. And not too long. Sister Felicity, come.

SISTER FELICITY. *(To LITTLE JOHN in passing.)* Sinner. *(They go out.)*

ROBIN. *(To LITTLE JOHN and WILL SCARLET.)* You two can wait outside. I see how well you keep my secrets. Go on, it's all right. *(They go out sheepishly.)*

MARIAN. You mustn't be cross with them. It's not their fault. Why did you not wish to see me?

ROBIN. I prefer being sick in private.

MARIAN. Are you very sick? Your wound?

ROBIN. Nothing mortal, I fear.

MARIAN. Then what's wrong? Why aren't you in the forest with your men?

ROBIN. I do far less harm here. The King is off to fight more wars, Prince John is looting villages. I think it's time I disappeared.

MARIAN. You can't disappear, there's people need you. Is it the killing? All right, you killed the Sheriff. He's tried to kill you many times, he would have killed you then. What kind of hero are you, anyway?

ROBIN. Is that your vision of a proper hero? One who jumps about hacking up his enemies and shooting arrows through people's heads? If that's a hero, I don't care to be one.

MARIAN. And just what do you care to be?

ROBIN. My father was a foul-tempered man, taught me to fight. Taught me too well, as it turned out. Plowing in a field, he was, and taunting me about a woman I'd a fancy for and he did not. I spoke rudely to him and he struck me, and I struck back. I would have thought the man possessed a thicker head than that, but it cracked like an egg. And now I've killed again, and by and by I'll kill another time. It's a disease one does not cure.

MARIAN. You'll kill yourself if you stay cooped up here.

ROBIN. No, the Prioress will do it for me. She's poisoning me, bit by bit. Prince John's paid her off. He cannot take me here in sanctuary, so the woman feeds me poison.

MARIAN. My God, why do you stay, then? Are you eating that? *(He has in fact been eating as he talks.)* Stop that. STOP IT.

ROBIN. It's of no consequence. I've thought it through. A cheerful pagan death is fine with me. *(He drinks.)*

MARIAN. What's that you're drinking?

ROBIN. Poison, I think. The woman seems to have decided to finish me today—tastes awful.

MARIAN. *(Jerking the glass away from him and throwing it out the window.)* DON'T DRINK THAT.

(From out the window, a cow moos indignantly.)

MARIAN. LITTLE JOHN.

(LITTLE JOHN sticks his head in the window.)

LITTLE JOHN. Yes, miss?

MARIAN. Go fetch the Prioress, force her to make an antidote to what she's poisoned Robin with. And make her drink it first. Don't ask me questions now, just do it please. *(LITTLE JOHN'S head disappears.)*

ROBIN. You're a bit too late, I think. *(He staggers towards the bed.)*

MARIAN. I WILL NOT HAVE YOU DYING. I WON'T ALLOW IT. HELP. WILL SCARLET. WILL.

(WILL SCARLET appears.)

WILL SCARLET. What is it? Is he poorly?

MARIAN. Help me lay him on the bed. *(They get ROBIN on the bed, his head on a pillow.)*

ROBIN. Will, you must do me a favor, now, listen. Take my bow and shoot an arrow in the air, and watch where it lands. Wherever that my be, bury me there, will you do that for me?

WILL SCARLET. Yes, Robin, I will.

ROBIN. Go and do it now, then. *(WILL hesitates, looks at MARIAN, then goes.)*

MARIAN. I forbid you to die. I forbid it.

(LITTLE JOHN drags in the PRIORESS.)

LITTLE JOHN. The woman says she's got an antidote.

PRIORESS. Oh, Robin, I'm so sorry, but I couldn't help it, I feared they'd burn us out and kill my girls.

ROBIN. What you've done I have allowed you.

PRIORESS. Here's the antidote. *(She holds out a vile looking yellow liquid in a bottle.)*

LITTLE JOHN. I made her drink some first, but still she may be lying.

MARIAN. Drink it. You must get well. If you care at all for me then do not argue, drink it.

ROBIN. Well, if you put it that way. Cheers. *(He drinks.)* Judas Priest, it tastes worse than the poison. What IS this? Vinegar and goat piss?

PRIORESS. Well, yes, it is. But it doth work, I swear.

(GWENNY and GUMMY GRANNY are at the door.)

GWENNY. Can we come in?

ROBIN. Gwenny? How did you get here?

GWENNY. Followed Miss Marian, who followed Little John. Say hello, Granny.

OLD GUMMY GRANNY. Whoodle, whoodle, Robby Hudd.

GWENNY. She made you this quilt here, heard you was poorly.

ROBIN. *(As they put the quilt around him.)* It's a fine quilt, it is.

(EADOM appears with a rubber chicken.)

EADOM. It's me too, Robin, Eadom. I've brung a chicken to make soup for you—I know you dislike killing living things to eat, but do not scold me, this one is all right, the chicken died of natural causes, it died a choking on a weasel turd, I swear.

ROBIN. Thank you, Eadom, I'll keep that in mind.

(ELLEN appears with JENNY.)

ELLEN. We come too, Robin, me and Jenny, we been so worried about you.

(They are all crowding in now, ALAN and DAVEY, WILL STUTELY and QUIGLEY. FLINT wheels himself in, zoom.)

FLINT. WHEEEEEEEEEEEEE—oops.
EADOM. Watch it Flint, you'll break my legs.
FLINT. Sorry, brakes is out of whack. Also, it's kinda fun.

(SISTER FELICITY comes running back in, hysterical.)

SISTER FELICITY. Oh, Mother, help. I can't keep 'em all out, they's everyplace, the dirty people, it's like a parade.

FLINT. We all come to see you, Robin. Mitch the Miller, Bell the Tinker, Cootie the Drunk, even Friar Tuck—

FRIAR TUCK. Speak civil, Flint, or I'll sit on you.

JENNY. They said you was dyin', Robin, but we knew it was a lie.

ROBIN. I'd think you all would hate me now, the way Prince John's been tearing up the countryside.

GWENNY. Ain't your fault the rich treat us like dirt. They always did, it ain't because of you, it's 'cause I don't know why, maybe if we was them we'd act the same. We don't expect our hero folk to win, Robin, that ain't a very realistic wish—we just expect them now and then to kind of act the part. We love you, sir.

ROBIN. Gwenny, you shame me.

(WILL SCARLET comes rushing in.)

WILL SCARLET. Let me by. Let me by. I've done the deed, Robin, I've shot the arrow.

ROBIN. And where did it come down?

WILL SCARLET. Well, that is the curious part, you see, it didn't exactly come down at all.

ROBIN. It must have come down, Will.

WILL SCARLET. It didn't fall, I swear, it went up, and up, and up into a cloud and disappeared.

ROBIN. In a cloud.

WILL SCARLET. It did. I swear it did. I never lie—well, not to you I don't.

ROBIN. You swear upon your soul the arrow did not come down?

WILL SCARLET. I swear.

ROBIN. Well, then. I suppose I will just have to live forever. Or at least until the thing comes down.

WILL SCARLET. That seems fair to me.

ROBIN. Do you know, Prioress, I'm feeling remarkably better. My compliments to the goat. Marian, my dear, would you like to take a walk with me? Into the woods, and the fresh air?

MARIAN. I would like to, yes.

ROBIN. It is earlier in the year, perhaps, than I had thought. *(He has managed to get up, and as the people chatter at them and help them off, LITTLE JOHN takes WILL SCARLET to one side.)*

LITTLE JOHN. Listen, Will, tell me true, now, did the arrow really not come down?

WILL SCARLET. Not that I seen.

LITTLE JOHN. But Will, how could a arrow not come down? I mean, you shoots it up and it comes down, you shoots it up and it comes down—I shot a million arrows in my time and never one I shot that went up did not come down.

WILL SCARLET. To be honest with you, Johnny, what I did, see, I tied the arrow to a dove's foot, and then I shot it gentle into the air, dove and all, so soft did I do it, John, it was a thing of beauty, and up she went, into the air, with arrow tied to foot, and flew off far into the sky, and thus did not come down. She must be flying still.

LITTLE JOHN. Even so, she's got to come down some time, you know, Will.

WILL SCARLET. Not where I can see it. And if she does, we'll have to bury Robin Hood alive, for frankly, Johnny, I don't think he's of a mind to die today. *(As they go off with the others, ALAN sings.)*

ALAN.

SO MANY A YEAR DID ROBIN HOOD
IN SHERWOOD FOREST DWELL
AND SOME DO SAY THAT IN THE WOODS
THE MAN IS LIVING STILL
AMONG THE LEAVES AND TANGLED VINES
AMONG THE TWISTED TREES
IF YOU LISTEN LOVE YOU STILL MAY HEAR
THE ANCIENT MELODIES,
THE ANCIENT MELODIES.

INDEX OF MUSIC

There are nine songs in *Robin Hood,* and internal passages from some of them appear as refrains in various parts of the play. When you come to a song in the text, check this index to find the melody that goes with those words, then check the music and find the words to discover which passages in the melody they are to be sung to.

MUSIC FOR ROBIN HOOD

THE MONTHS OF THE YEAR

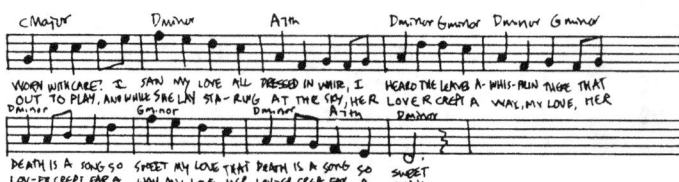

MARIAN'S SONG

Dminor   Aminor   Dminor   A7th

WITH- IN THE FOR-EST DARK AND DEEP, A— MONG THE GNARLED AND TWISTED WOODS A-
I MET A DEAD MAN IN THE WOOD I MET THE DE —VIL ON THE HILL, I

Dminor   Gminor   Dminor   Gminor Dminor   Dminor

-MONG THE FAL-LEN CHERRY TREES THE LADY SITS A- LONE AND BROODS. I WISH YOU WERE
MET MY TRUE LOVE COLD AND WHITE, UP- ON HER LIPS IT WAS SO CHILL MY FATH-ER HE

IN THE WILD- WOOD DEEP, I WISH YOU WERE IN THE SEA — I WISH YOU WERE
HAD AN ACRE OF LAND, DOWN BY— THE OCEAN SEA HE SOWED IT WITH

Gminor   Dminor Gminor

IN THE BOT-TOM OF HELL AND FAR A— WAY FROM ME — AND FAR A—WAY FROM
BONES AND WA-TERED WITH BLOOD ALL UN-EE KNOWNT TO ME — ALL— UN-BE-KNOWNST TO

Dminor

ME —
ME —

GIFTS GIVEN

Aminor   Dminor   Aminor   GMajor Aminor

WHAT WILL YOU LEAVE TO YOUR BRO-THER JOHN? THE GA-AL-OWS TRE—EE TO HANG HIM ON

Dminor   Aminor   Dminor E7th

WHAT WILL YOU LEAVE TO YOUR BRO-THER'S WIFE? THE WIL-DER- NE-ESS TO END HER LIFE.

Aminor   Dminor   Aminor   Dminor   E7th

WHAT WILL YOU LEAVE TO THE WOODS SO GREEN? I WILL MAKE IT IN-TO A DES-ERT

Aminor

LAND

LONELY SONG

I CANNOT SEE HER WESTWARD, I, CANNOT SEE HER SOUTH I CANNOT TOUCH MY
TRUE LOVE NOW, I, CANNOT KISS HER MOUTH. AND LONELY IS THE GRASSY GLENN AND LONELY IS THE
SEA, AND LONELY IS THE WILD WOOD DEEP WHEN SHE IS GONE FROM ME - WHEN SHE IS GONE FROM ME

THE SONG OF THE TUXFORD MAIDENS

OHHHHH, WE ARE THREE MAIDS OF TUX-FORD WE SING A TUX-FORD SONG, THAT LIFE IS VE-RY
SHORT MY LOVE AND DEATH IS VER-Y LONG — WE LOVE TO ROMP A- MONG THE TREES AND PLAY WITH ALL THE BIRR-WE'D
WHEN-EV-ER WE FEEL BLUE AND GRAY AND LICE CREEP THROUGH OUR HAIR- WE
LIKE TO SAY OUR PRAYER FOR YOU BUT WE FOR-GOT THE WORDS. OHH! GOD HELP THE POOR AND SICK, GOD
RUB ON YE OLDE FUZ-ZO AND BE-FORE LONG WE DONT CARE. OHH! GOD HELP THE OLD AND FRAIL, THE
BLESS THE WEAK AND YEARNING AND GO-D HELP THE FIL-THY RICH WHEN THEY IN HELL ARE BURN-ING
HUNG-RY AND FOR-GOTTEN, FOR HELL BE TOR-TUR-ING THE RICH WHEN YOU AND I ARE ROT-TEN

THE DEVIL SONG

HELP ME TO YOUR WINE, SHE SAID, LET ME SING MY SONG
LIFE IS VE-RY SHORT, SHE SAID, DEATH IS VE-RY LONG

THE QUEEN OF POVERTY

I AM THE QUEEN OF PO-VER-TY I AM PRINCESS OF NEED I SING MY SONG AND NO ONE HEARS, THE WORLD IS MADE OF GREED THE WORLD IS MADE OF GREED

THREE RAVENS

AS I WAS WALKIN SO LONE-LY, I SAW THREE RA-VENS IN A TREE, THEY WAS AS BLACK AS BLACK COULD BE WITH A DOWNE DERRY DERRY DORRY DOWNE
WHERE SHALL WE DINE TO DAY SAYS ONE? DOWN YONDER WHERE THE WIL-LOW BROOK DOES RUN THERE LIES A DEAD MAN IN THE SUN WITH A DOWNE DERRY DOWNE

A RIDDLING SONG

OH WHAT IS GREENER THAN THE GRASS AND WHAT IS HIGHER THAN THE TREES? OR WHAT IS WORSE THAN WOMANS WISH A-ND WHA-AT IS DE-EE-PER THA-AN THE SEAS?
DEATH IS GREENER THAN THE GRASS AND HEAVEN'S HIGHER THAN THE TREES, THE DEV-IL'S WORSE THAN WOMANS WISH A-ND HE-LL IS DE-EE-PER THA-AN THE SEAS.

AFTERWORD

Notes On *ROBIN HOOD*

I
(On Robin as Archetype)

It has been suggested by various persons that there really was a historical Robin Hood, who roamed the English countryside some time between the twelfth and fourteenth centuries, robbing the rich and giving to the poor, or perhaps robbing everybody and keeping the loot for himself. It has also been argued that Robin was a fabrication of story-tellers, balladeers and medieval playwrights. Margaret Murray asserts in *The God of the Witches* that Robin Hood is one manifestation of Robin Goodfellow, behind whose fairly benign characterization in *Midsummer Night's Dream* lies a darker history as an ancient pagan horned wood god who became, as Christianity spread through northern Europe and Great Britain, the Devil himself.

What may be a sticky problem for historians, folklorists and students of religion is fortunately not a problem for the playwright, who is a liar by profession and for whom all these explanations are true, as well as any others which he may care to imagine. The playwright turns everything to myth, and myth into ritual, gives the Word flesh, puts the archetype in motion — puts it, in short, upon a stage, where Robin may be at least as real as a character who carries the name of a documented historical figure like Prince John. The question for the

114

playwright is not so much, Was there a Robin Hood and what was he like? as What face will Robin wear in this particular dramatic incarnation in this particular universe?

It is in the nature of such archetypal figures that they change over the centuries as our perception of them changes — they are, in a sense, what each era is capable of perceiving them to be. Enough qualities are carried over from one manifestation to another to keep the character recognizable as the same figure from one century to the next — the Odysseus of Homer is and is not the Odysseus of Sophocles and the Ulysses of Shakespeare, Tennyson and Joyce. Of the many traditional characteristics of Robin Hood, some of those which one might find most compelling are his obsession with the forest, his feeling of connectedness to animals and trees, his alienation from society and from the wealthy and powerful, his sense of humor, his gentlemanly behavior, his compassion for the poor, his disinclination towards violence when other options are available. But one might just as easily have chosen to emphasize other qualities and made a quite different Robin. There are hints, for example, in the earlier stories, of a more bloodthirsty and amoral figure. And even when Robin is portrayed as ultimately benign, it is in part that fear of the outlaw and outcast who lives in dark forbidden places that makes him so interesting to us, and so effective at what he does. There is a definite relationship between the sense of freedom he represents and the feeling of danger connected to that freedom. An outlaw in medieval England was by definition one who could be killed without penalty.

One pays a price for freedom, and for being different from one's neighbors, more committed to a certain course of action, to a certain moral position — one becomes a symbol and is trapped finally in the world of the archetypal hero.

The archetype is flexible, and he endures, and through the centuries he absorbs meaning like a sponge, becoming a richer symbol as he ages. The playwright makes lies like truth — his truth is not the truth of the journalist or the historian, although he respects and makes use of their findings when he needs them. His truth is the protean, enduring truth of the archetype, a special kind of lie which connects patterns in human experience from century to century, and which lives on when more circumstantial truths have been lost in the complex wreckage of time and chance.

II

(On Robin Hood and the Bogey of Anachronism, or, Why Costume Drama is Everything but *Oh, Calcutta.*)

Having been accused by more than one person of compulsively falling prey in my work to a terrible sin called Anachronism, and deeply ashamed of myself as I am, I've decided it's time to take a look at my sins and see if I can discover what they reveal about my own preconceptions about theatre, and how these preconceptions may differ from those of sane, right-thinking people of good taste everywhere. Now, anachronism (from the Greek *anachronismos,* that is, *ana-* (against) + *chronos* (time) is, according to my dictionary, the representation of something as existing or occurring at other than its proper time, especially earlier, or, anything out of its proper historical time.

For example, in *Pericles, Prince of Tyre,* the author, presumably Shakespeare or a reasonable facsimile therof, has the good citizens of ancient Ephesus or thereabouts toting muskets around with them. Now, as a rather well-read gentleman in ancient literature — Ben Jonson's comments about small Latin and less Greek notwithstanding — and a somewhat perceptive fellow, Shakespeare must have noticed that the ancient Greeks, if Plutarch and Herodotus are to be trusted, tended to get along quite nicely with a noticeable dearth of firearms. Those smug persons who explain such things by telling us that the Elizabethans had no sense of historical time are assuming rather more stupidity on the part of great playwrights than it seems to me the evidence warrants. Either we presume, like certain Victorian gentlemen, that Shakespeare and his cohorts, Godlike as they may have been in other respects, were in the matter of history rather precocious but not very observant children, or we must consider the possibility that one's reasons for placing muskets in the hands of the ancients might have more to do with dramaturgical and practical theatre choices than with a stupendous ignorance of history.

In any case, such a Periclean musket would be a genuine anachronism, a thing out of its proper historical time. One might conclude that this is largely a matter of convenience, as the Elizabethan custom seems to have been more often than not to costume everybody in more or less contemporary clothing, the anachronism being, as it were, built into Elizabethan stage convention. If so, then the proper time of Elizabethan drama was not the same as the proper time of a historian's view of an era depicted in a given play, and those who are distressed by such anachronisms are actually, unbeknownst to themselves, trying to apply one set of conventions (often in modern times associated with words like 'realism' and 'naturalism') to dramatic universes to which they were never meant to apply. 'Realism' is not synonymous with 'reality'. What we usually call 'realism' in the theatre is simply a set of conventions like any other set of conventions.

Of course, the play is real in the sense that real actors are performing before a real audience (well, this is at least a commonly accepted level of reality, although we may check in with Prospero later for an alternative view) but the play only represents, with a series of conventions, the story it is telling. A play may represent an infinite number of realities in an infinite number of ways. And in this sense any play is itself one giant anachronism — a universe being recreated out of its proper time — for it is by definition never exactly the time it is supposed to represent. So if we can't have absolute reality in theatre, do we then decide that the next best thing is at least some sort of consistency? Well, what kind?

If a play is set in Germany, must everybody speak German? If not, then already we have accepted a very unrealistic convention. Observe the movies struggling with such dilemmas in innumerable pictures about the Second World War. Do the Germans speak German to each other and English to the English? Then how do we understand what the Germans are saying to each other? Well, we can have subtitles — another highly unrealistic convention — a level of reading reality superimposed upon a level of picture reality — or we can decide that the Germans will always speak English, even though the convention we are tacitly accepting is that they are 'really' speaking English with the English and German with the Germans, but then, do we give them German accents? And if they always speak with German accents, what does that mean? Since the convention is that they're really speaking German to the other Germans, why does it sound the same as when they're speaking English to the English, and why, for that matter, do they have accents at all? And if they sound just like the English, all the time, then that is yet another convention — and if we see a Nazi out of uniform, how do we know if he is really supposed to be speaking German or English? And all the while we also know perfectly well that these Germans aren't real Germans, they're an Irishman named O'Toole and a Swede named Max who once played Jesus in another movie, but we don't turn in horror and say, "My God, Mabel, Jesus is a Nazi." We accept these rather bizarre and complex conventions so we can watch the movie without going insane, and even consider it to be fairly 'realistic.'

You may be wondering, at this point, what all this has got to do with Robin Hood. Well, if a play is set, say, in the past, in England, must the characters speak the English of the period depicted? The further back from our period we go, the more English begins to sound to us like gibberish. So what do we want? A play with subtitles? Or just something that is recognizably English but that sounds kind of quaint, a generalized kind of archaic-sounding speech? And this brings us to 'Costume drama,' which is a mildly derogatory term sometimes used to describe a kind of generalized archaic play which attempts to coordinate its anachronisms in a relatively non-threatening way.

The literary manager of a famous and well-respected resident nonprofit theatre reads and is excited by a play which happens to feature Shakespeare, Marlowe, and several other Elizabethan people, a play written by a contemporary, undead playwright. The literary manager goes to the artistic director, a very powerful and respected gentleman, and urges him to read this play, which seems to him very superior to most of the plays they receive. But the artistic director glances at the cast of characters and refuses categorically to read it. "We don't do costume drama." he says.

Now, what does this man really mean? Presumably he doesn't mean that his theatre does only nudist drama, as nearly all the people in all of the plays his theatre has produced have to the best of my knowledge worn costumes of one sort or another most of the time. And it can't mean that they don't do plays set in the past, as he has done over the years many interesting productions of plays written by Shakespeare and other dead people from Europe. So this unfortunately rather typical response must mean, as near as I can make out, that he considers any play by a living American playwright not set in the present or the very recent past to fall into a category of beast called 'costume drama,' a phrase which conjures up images of people staggering about in ridiculously overpadded costumes hopefully unlike anything anybody in the past was ever actually stupid enough to wear, reciting impossibly dull and seemingly endless, incredibly stilted speeches in extraordinarily bad blank verse or a kind of generic oldtime snoot-language popular in Errol Flynn movies. This, as near as I can figure, is what the distinguished gentleman meant by 'costume drama,' and in a way one can't blame him much, as I wouldn't want to go and see a play like that, either. His not very hidden presumption is that living playwrights in his country should only be writing contemporary plays in the realistic tradition — nothing else is really serious writing, at least if it's by an American. This is of course the same institutional stupidity that faced realistic playwrights in the late nineteenth century, who were struggling with a theatre establishment which thought that plays MUST take place in some sort of highly artificial and romantic past to be serious plays. This institutional bigotry is a feature of every age — the conventions which are popular, trendy or respectable at any given time may vary, but the attitude of those distinguished arbiters of taste is always more or less the same: a serious play can only be one of these. If it's not one of these, then it must be one of those, and we don't do those, because those are obviously not serious plays, because we don't do them. If it is about this, or employs these conventions, it is by definition not worth our attention, unless of course it was written by someone now long dead, in which case it maybe is a classic, which is of course an entirely different thing. Most playwrights ultimately either conform to the fashionable prejudices of these morons, take up some other line of work, go insane or kill themselves in order to improve their chances of production. The few survivors, like Shakespeare, quietly go about the business of developing a set of conventions which suits the stories they want to tell, and which in turn will be used to oppress later generations of playwrights once the old boy is safely packed away in the sod and his works are safely in the hands of the succeeding theatre establishment, most of whose distinguished members would not have given him bus fare to the bathroom when he was alive.

Well, then, look, if every play is a collection of conventions and a giant anachronistic mechanism, does this mean that I may with great impunity put television sets in Henry the Eighth's bedroom and dinosaurs in Pittsburgh? Of course I can, and although this doesn't mean the resulting play is going to be any good (the odds are against it, because the odds are always against any attempt to create anything) it also does not mean that it will necessarily be bad: *Julius Caesar* has lovely anachronisms sprouting up here and there all over it like mushrooms, while Ben Jonson's *Sejanus* is much more consistently archaic — but the former remains a rather lively piece of theatre when done with some imagination, while the latter has for centuries been noted as a kind of Elizabethan form of Sominex. Anachronism is in itself neither a virtue nor a vice — it is simply a fact of theatrical convention, recognized or not. When you are engaged in making theatre, you are employing a variety of ancient conventions of one sort or another, even if it seems to you

that you are inventing them as you go along, and you are
also generating an anachronistic mechanism — and that
is, in part, the real joy of it.

A.E. Housman suggests that a good poem is one that
gives you goose bumps and a chill, that raises the hackles
on the back of one's neck, and I must confess that *King
Lear* usually does this to me, but then, so does the theme
music to *The Twilight Zone* — my psyche remembering an
intense viewing experience it had when I was twelve.
Whether a play is a good play or not tends to depend on
who you are talking to and when you are talking to them,
but whether one likes a given play or not, it seems to me
intensely stupid to deny the simple truth that a play is
first of all a piece of literature. It is a kind of literature
meant to be read and then acted out, just as the songs of
Burns and the Robin Hood ballads are kinds of literature
meant to be read and then sung, and *Moby-Dick* is a kind
of literature meant to be read and imagined in the
reader's head. To insist that plays are not literature is to
confuse a play with its production. The play is a fictional
universe written down, and a fictional universe that is
written down is literature, and the fact of a play's being
the written down part of a production is not something to
be sneezed at, because what is written down is what
endures when the production is over and all the people
who saw it are dead. This is not to suggest that unscripted
theatrical events are any less interesting as theatrical
events, or that most plays are very complex or rewarding
literature — just that the thing I am spending my life
doing is making universes on paper that can be
transformed magically under the proper conditions into

living flesh in places where I'll never go, for people I will never meet, in the manner of Euripides and Shakespeare and Chekhov, all of us making fictional universes out of words and therefore making literature, as much as Yeats or Faulkner or Dante.

The blueprint theory of drama is true enough as far as it goes — it only becomes false when it becomes reductive. To observe that a play is a blueprint for action on a stage is perfectly true. To say that a play is 'merely' a blueprint for production is as meaningful as to say that *War and Peace* is 'merely' a blueprint for what you are to imagine happening in your head. The 'merely', spoken or implied, is what's misleading. The play is reincarnated in successive productions as the soul in Hindu mythology is reincarnated in successive bodies. The play is the soul of the production, the part that is potentially, in a manner of speaking, immortal. In a play you can go anywhere and do anything, and this is true precisely because a play is a set of moving symbolic conventions. *Miss Julie* may be an example of a set of conventions you would like to call 'realism' or 'naturalism,' but it is ultimately no more or less real than *King Lear* or *Waiting for Godot* or *Le Voyage de Monsieur Perrichon*. In a play, a girl walks out onto a bare stage and announces, 'Here we are in sunny Spain!' and if she is doing her job well, and if the audience is disposed to cooperate, she will create that reality for them, or they will create it together. We are dealing here in living archetypes, patterns in human experience which recur again and again in slightly different 'costume,' as it were, and there are an infinite number of such costumes and such conventions, and when we allow fashionable bigotry to blind us to this multiplicity of possibilities in theatre we are making ourselves systematically stupid.

III
(On the Worship of Death
and the Theatre as Robin Hood.)

The single most tragic fact about American theatre is that it has been tied for so long to the goals of financial speculators and the accumulation of capital by people who already have more than they can use that it has been extremely difficult for Americans to see theatre as anything more than a frivolous and rather trivial relaxation, or to think of it in other terms than those two monuments to cretinism, the "hit" and the "flop." — these being code words perpetuated by reviewers and other persons prone to extreme fluctuations between sycophancy and cannibalism and ultimately being synonymous with the good capitalist words "profit" and "loss." A hit is a play that generates profit. A flop is a play that does not. To use words like this is to buy into a Fascist mentality that has for two centuries managed to successfully murder most attempts to create a serious theatre in this country. Reviews are about money, not art. Praise and blame are illusions. Theatre is about something else entirely.

This same authoritarian mentality that has crippled the arts in America has savaged the environment mercilessly, operating under much the same logic: the deadly illusion that a thing only has value if it can generate profits. The result of this reasoning has been a pollution and butchery of the earth unparalleled in human history — and a perpetuation of poverty and ignorance in the service of that same vile and murderous set of authoritarian ideologies. They try to censor what we read and see and write, to control what we think, to convince us that sex is evil, they promote deadly and insane technologies that lend themselves to control by a few giant corporations. They have made an alliance with death. And the true theatre, which is life and joy and is an expression of human freedom and communion, will always be the enemy of these people, will always be persecuted, ridiculed, and feared by them, will always be the outlaw. But it won't die.

PROPERTIES/FURNITURE

SCENE ONE:
Picnic basket with:
    Grapes, salami, bread, apples, etc.
Blanket
Brooch — Maid Marion
Staff — Friar Tuck
Broadswords — Merry Men
Finger on string around neck — Watt

SCENE TWO:
Huge throne for Prince John
Regular throne for Bronwen
Wheel chair for Queen Eleanor
Table — collapsible
Map — Prince John
Pillow — Yorick
Candy — Bronwen
Sack — Yorick
Tray with:
    Toenail polish
Silver tray service with:
    Teapot, cups, napkins, spoons

SCENE THREE:
Two stools/stumps
Trunk with gowns and lingerie
Six bowls
Kettle with beans, hanging from tree

Ladle
Rag
Herbs
Six spoons
Checklist with quill — Will Stutely
Assorted bows and arrows and quivers

SCENE FOUR:
Large table
Two benches
Two stools
Rolling keg with six mugs
Broom — Jenny
Rag — Jenny
Bucket and rag — Ellen
Tarot cards — Betty
Mug — Cootie
Staff — Monk
Wooden spoon — Eadom
Shawl — Ellen

SCENE FIVE:
Two stumps/stools
Quilt — Maid Marion
Rag dress
Paper and quill

SCENE SIX:
Huge throne
Regular throne
Wheelchair

Wastebasket
Table with:
  Map, breakaway bottle, goblet
Real peach — Bronwen
Horn — Grok

SCENE SEVEN:
Squares of cloth — Gummy Granny
Quilt
Flint's cart, handblocks

SCENE EIGHT:
Sign, "Purvis the Pedlar"
"I AM DUMM" sign
Twelve "Ye Olde Fuzzo" bottles
Plastic fruit and vegetables to throw

SCENE NINE:
Small table
Two stools
Jacks and ball — Stephen

SCENE TEN:
Huge throne
Regular throne
Nailfile — Bronwen
Silver tray service
Cloth message — Watt

SCENE ELEVEN:
Two trumpets
Long scroll with weighted end

SCENE TWELVE:
Two stumps/stools
Quill and paper
Staff — Monk

SCENE THIRTEEN:
Two trumpets
Wheelchair
Flint's cart
Big knife — Queen Eleanor
Swords — Merry Men, Richard

SCENE FOURTEEN:
Large table
Two benches
Two stools
Rolling keg
Bucket and mop — Ellen
Broom — Jenny
Six mugs
Quill and paper — Stutely

SCENE FIFTEEN:
Two benches for the bed
Quilt
Two stools
Tray with:
    Bowl of Irish stew, spoon, mug
Bottle of antidote
Rubber chicken
Flint's cart
Bow and arrows — Scarlet
Pillow

COSTUME PLOT

NOTE: Because the legend of Robin Hood developed over a period of about 600-800 years, any or all costume periods are appropriate, so long as they are "old-ish." It is suggested that most costumes reflect a time prior to 1800.

— Bitsy Bidwell, Costume Designer.

Alan a'Dale:

> Scene 1: Hat, shirt, jerkin, knee pants, stockings (tights, high boots, cape, belt with dagger, lute.
>
> Scene 3, 4, 5, 7, 8, 9, 10, 11, 12, 14, and 16: Same.
>
> Scene 13: Same. Add voluminous cape with hood for "old lady."

Sheriff of Nottingham:

> All scenes: Chain mail hood, helmet, shirt, padded leather jerkin (armor), pants, padded leather leg guards, short boots, belt, sword belt(s), leather gauntlets.

Marian:

> Scene 1: Dress, corset, petticoats, stockings, slippers, belt with purse, hat with gorget, cape.
>
> Scene 5: Quilt. Then.....
> "Set of Rags": Underdress, laced over-tunic, bare feet and legs.

Scenes 7, 9, 10: Same as Scene 5.

Scene 12: Dress, corset, petticoats, stockings, slippers, belt, cape.

Scene 13: Same as Scene 12.

Scene 14: Dress, corset, petticoats, stockings, slippers, same cape as in Scene 12 and 13.

Scene 15: Same as Scene 14.

Mistress Quigley:
All scenes: Blouse, laced bodice, corset, skirt, petticoats, stockings, slippers, cape with hood, cap, parasol.

Constable Watt:
All scenes: Chain mail hood and collar, shirt, padded leather vest with insignia of the Sheriff, knee pants, stockings, boots, gauntlets, sword belt, and belt.

Gill Redcap:
All scenes: Chain mail hood and collar, shirt, padded leather vest with insignia of the Sheriff, bound leggings, pants, stockings, soft shoes, sword belt, belt, bow, quiver, gauntlets.

Diccon Cruikshank:
All scenes: Chain mail hood and collar, shirt, pad-

ded leather jerkin with insignia of the Sheriff, chain mail leggings, stockings, boots, sword belt, belt, gauntlets.

Robin Hood/"Old Lady":
Scene 1: Voluminous dress with quick-opening front, wimple, hat, gorget. Then.......

Hat with feather, hood with collar, shirt, laced leather vest, knee pants, stockings, high boots, sword belt, belt, quiver and bow.

Scenes 3, 4, 5, 7, 12, and 13: Same as second part of Scene 1.

Scene 15: Remove hat, hood, quiver, bow. Unlace the vest.

Will Scarlet:
Scene 1: Hat with red feather, hood with collar, shirt, jerkin, knee pants, stockings, boots, quiver, bow, sword belt, belt, gauntlets, short cape.

Scene 3, 4, 5, 7, 12, 14, 15: Same.

Scene 13: Same. Add voluminous cape for "old lady."

Little John:
Scene 1: Cap, hood with collar, shirt, leather vest, knee pants, stockings, boots, quiver, bow, sword

belt, belt, gauntlets.

Scenes 3, 4, 5, 7, 12, 14, 15: Same.

Scene 13: Same. Add voluminous cape for "old lady."

Davy O'Doncaster:
Scene 1: Hat, shirt, vest, knee pants, stockings, boots, quiver, bow, sword belt, belt, gauntlets.

Scenes 3, 5, 7, 12, 14, 15: Same.

Scene 13: Same. Add voluminous cape for "old lady."

Will Stutely:
Scene 1: Cap, shirt, jerkin, knee pants, stockings, boots, quiver, bow, sword belt, belt, gauntlets.

Scenes 3, 5, 12, 14, 15: Same.

Scene 13: Same. Add voluminous cape for "old lady."

Friar Tuck:
Scene 1: Tonsured hair, robe, belt with purse, rosary, dagger, stockings, boots, cape, and padding, if needed.

Scenes 3, 5, 7, 12, 14, 15: Same.

Scene 13: Same. Add voluminous cape for "old lady."

Bronwen:

Scene 2: Corset, low-cut underdress, overdress, petticoats, jeweled girdle, elaborate headdress, rings, bracelets, necklace, earrings, bare feet and legs.

Scene 6: Same as Scene 1.

Scene 10: Corset, low-cut dress with large jeweled sleeves, petticoats, jeweled stomacher, turban headdress, jewelry, belt with pomander, stockings, slippers.

Scene 13: Same dress as Scene 10 with trailing over-dress in Prince John's heraldic insignia, new jewelry, new headdress which apes a crown (but isn't), veil, stockings, slippers.

Yorick:

Scene 2: Jester's cap with bells and padding (for head-stands), collar with points, multi-colored jerkin and melon hose-pants, codpiece, par-ticolored stockings, puffed and slashed mis-matched slippers, morris bells, belt with various pouches.

Queen Eleanor:

Scene 2: Underdress, petticoats, overdress with

Prince John's heraldric insignia for decoration, elaborate sleeves with lace cuffs, several gauzy shawls, crown, several gauzy veils, jewelry, stockings, slippers.

Scene 6: Same.

Scene 13: Same underdress, overdress trimmed in ermine with standing ruff, jewelry, crown and scepter.

Sally:

Scene 2: Chemise, underdress, laced overdress, dishcloth for belt with small pouch, drooping socks, slippers, rag to hold back hair.

Scene 10: Same.

Prince John:

Scene 2: Crown, soft shirt, elaborate doublet with fur collar, knee pants, codpiece, stockings, puffed and slashed shoes, medallion of office, short shoulder cape, sword belt and ornamental sword, rings.

Scene 6: Same as Scene 2.

Scene 10: Same crown, soft shirt, another doublet, stockings (cross gartered), soft shoes, cape, jewelry, same sword and belt.

Scene 13: New crown and scepter. Same doublet,
etc. as Scene 10 with addition of over-tabard in his
own heraldic insignia, remove cross garters, soft
shoes.

Jenny:
All scenes: Shirt, skirt, laced corselette bodice,
overskirt, bare feet.

Ellen:
All scenes: Chemise, overdress, belt with dishcloth,
laced vest, bare feet.

Crazy Betty:
All scenes: Ragged dress, several ragged skirt
overlayers, cape with hood, soft shoes.

Eadom:
All scenes: Too-small shirt tied together with string
over potbelly, knee pants, stockings, ankle boots,
string belt and dishcloth.

Cootie the Drunk:
All scenes: Shirt, vest, knee pants, stockings, soft
shoes, belt, cape, cap.

Dark Monk/Richard:
Scene 4: Monk's robe with oversize cuffs, collar
with oversize hood, cord belt, stockings, shoes,
staff.

Scenes 7 and 12: Same.

Scene 13: Same robe, etc. as above with following dressed underneath for quick reveal — helmet with skull face, doublet, shirt, pumpkin pants, stockings, boots, cape, sword belt and sword, medallion of office, jewelry.

Grok:

All scenes: Jester's hat with attached collar, jerkin, stockings, leggings, soft pointed shoes, bauble, belt.

Gwenny:

All scenes: Extremely ragged dress in several layers, filthy, patched with neat fabric squares, stringy headband, bare feet.

Gummy Granny:

All scenes: Extremely ragged blouse, vest, skirt, filthy, patched with neat fabric squares, ragged wimple and gorget, staff, bare feet.

Flint:

All scenes: Extremely ragged shirt draped onto straw on board, jaunty ragged cap.

Purvis the Peddler:

All scenes: Hat, collar with hood, jerkin, knee pants, stockings, thigh-high boots, gauntlets, belt with pouches and dagger.

Blind Benny, Deaf Danny, Dumb Duggan:
> All scenes: Matching ragged tabards held with cord belts. Blind Benny has a cloth over his eyes. Ragged shirts, knee pants, stockings, soft shoes.

Three Maids of Tuxford:
> Scene 8: First (young) maids: Matching chemise dresses held by cord belts, bare feet.

> Scene 8: Second (old) maids: Identical matching shemise dresses, very ragged and dirty, no belts, bare feet.

Sam the Rag:
> All scenes: Ragged shirt, tunic, knee pants, bare legs and feet, belt.

Mitch the Miller:
> All scenes: Ragged jerkin, knee pants, vest, stockings, soft boots, cape, belt.

Bell the Tinker:
> All scenes: Ragged shirt, knee pants, vest, stockings, soft boots, cape, belt.

Arthur O'Bland:
> All scenes: Ragged shirt, vest, knee pants, leggings, soft shoes, cape, cap, belt.

Sir Stephen:
> Scene 9: Large hat, shirt, jerkin, mellon-hose pants,

coat with fur collar, stockings, shoes with points
held up by chains to knees, medallion, rings, belt
with jacks, pouch and small dagger.

Brekka:

Scene 10: Babushka, kerchief at neck, blouse,
basque-bodice vest, underskirt, petticoats, overskirt, stockings, soft shoes.

Ghost:

Scene 15: Duplicate of Robin's outfit only ragged,
with blood stains, worn underneath Dark Monk's
robe which has been opened up the front.

Prioress:

Scene 15: Black underdress, petticoats, black overdress with hanging bellows-sleeves, wimple, gorget, and headdress, belt with pouch and cross
hanging.

Sister Felicity:

Scene 15: Black robe with white cuffs, bibbed
apron, wimple, gorget, and headdress, rosary and
pouch on apron strings, petticoats, stockings,
soft shoes.

Various Peasants:

All scenes: Rags.

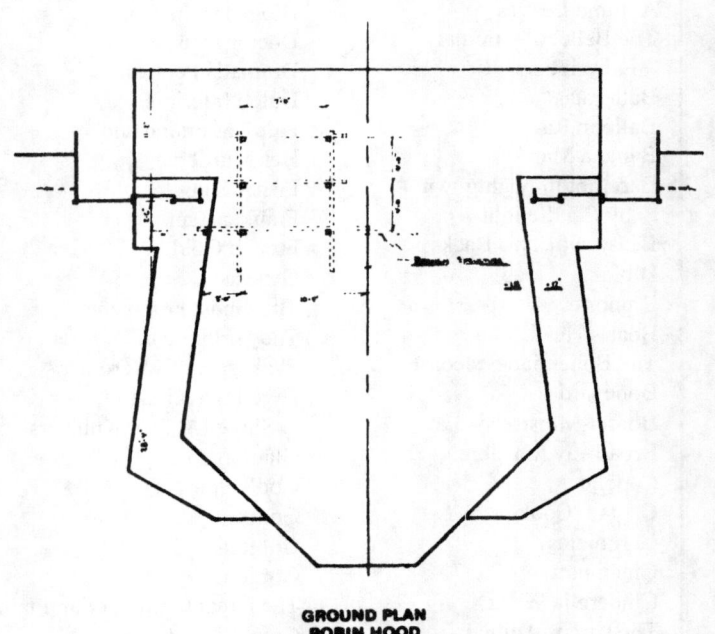

GROUND PLAN
ROBIN HOOD

Also by
Don Nigro...

Anima Mundi
Animal Salvation
Ardy Fafirsin
Armitage
Autumn Leaves
The Babel of Circular
  Labyrinths
Ballerinas
Balloon Rat
Banana Man
Barefoot in Nightgown
  by Candlelight
Beast with Two Backs
Bible
Binnorie
Boar's Head
The Bohemian Seacoast
Boneyard
Border Minstrelsy
Broadway Macabre
Capone
Captain Cook
Chronicles
Cincinnati
Cinderella Waltz
The Circus Animals'
  Desertion
Creatures Lurking in
  the Churchyard
Crossing the Bar
The Curate Shakespeare
  As You Like It
The Dark Sonnets of
  the Lady
The Dark
The Daughters of
  Edward D. Boit

The Dead Wife
The Death of Von Horvath
Deflores
The Devil
Diogenes the Dog
Doctor Faustus
Dramatis Personae
Dutch Interiors
Fair Rosamund and
  Her Murderer
Fisher King
Frankenstein
French Gold
Genesis
The Ghost Fragments
The Girlhood of
  Shakespeare's Heroines
Give Us a Kiss and
    Show Us Your Knickers
Glamorgan
God's Spies
Gogol
Golgotha
Gorgons
The Great Gromboolian Plain
Great Slave Lake
Green Man
Grotesque Lovesongs
The Gypsy Woman
Haunted
Hieronymus Bosch
Higgs Field
Horrid Massacre in Boston
Horse Farce
Ida Lupino in the Dark
The Irish Girl Kissed
  in the Rain

Joan of Arc in the Autumn
The King of the Cats
Laestrygonians
The Last of the Dutch Hotel
The Lost Girl
Loves Labours Wonne
Lucia Mad
Lucy and the Mystery of the
  Vine Encrusted Mansion
Lurker
MacNaughton's Dowry
Madeline Nude in the
  Rain Perhaps
Madrigals
Major Weir
The Malefactor's
  Bloody Register
Mariner
Mink Ties
Monkey Soup
Mooncalf
Mulberry Street
My Sweetheart's The
  Man in the Moon
Narragansett
Necropolis
Netherlands
Nightmare with Clocks
November
Paganini
Palestrina
Panther
Pendragon
Pendragon Plays
Picasso
Ragnarok

Rat Wives
Ravenscroft
The Reeves Tale
Rhiannon
Ringrose the Pirate
Robin Hood
The Rooky Wood
Scarecrow
Seance
Seascape with Sharks
  and Dancer
The Sin-Eater
Something in the Basement
Sorceress
Specter
Squirrels (Nigro)
Sudden Acceleration
Sycorax
Tainted Justice
The Tale of the Johnson Boys
Tales from the Red Rose Inn
Things That Go Bump
  in the Night
The Transylvanian Clockworks
Tristan
Uncle Clete's Toad
Warburton's Cook
The Weird Sisters
Widdershins
Wild Turkeys
Winchelsea Dround
Within the Ghostly
Mansion's Labyrinth
Wolfsbane
The Wonders of the
  Invisible World Revealed
The Woodman and the Goblins

Please visit our website **samuelfrench.com** for complete
descriptions and licensing information

www.ingramcontent.com/pod-product-compliance
Lightning Source LLC
Chambersburg PA
CBHW070616120726
47909CB00004B/1233